Wonderful?
He thought she was wonderful?
No man had ever said that to Monica.

To Venus? Yes. Always to Venus. As Venus she'd been called spectacular, exquisite, dazzling, gorgeous. Men had complimented her on everything from her eyes to her ankles. Adoration was a given, but after months living in this small town as Monica Dulane, not one man had complimented her or given her a second look, which was the way she wanted it to be.

JD had changed all that. Here was a man telling and showing her how wonderful he thought she was. Just the way she was. He wrapped his arms around her, pressing his solid form against her until she felt the evidence of his desire and her own body grew warm and wet with wanting. Yes, she wanted him. She opened her mouth to receive him further inside and his moan of pleasure was all the encouragement she needed. Monica snaked an arm around his neck. "This is probably a mistake."

"I don't make mistakes, just calculated risks."

"I'm a big risk."

"I can take whatever you give me."

Books by Dara Girard

Kimani Romance

Sparks
The Glass Slipper Project
Taming Mariella
Power Play
A Gentleman's Offer
Body Chemisty
Round the Clock
Words of Seduction
Pages of Passion
Beneath the Covers
All I Want Is You

DARA GIRARD

fell in love with storytelling at an early age. Her romance writing career happened by chance when she discovered the power of a happy ending. She is an award-winning author whose novels are known for their sense of humor, interesting plot twists and witty dialogue.

When she's not writing she enjoys spring mornings and autumn afternoons, French pastries, dancing to the latest hits and long drives.

Dara loves to hear from her readers. You can reach her at contactdara@daragirard.com or P.O. Box 10345, Silver Spring, MD 20914.

All I Want is YOU
DARA GIRARD

KIMANI
ROMANCE

To true friends

KIMANI PRESS™

Recycling programs
for this product may
not exist in your area.

ISBN-13: 978-0-373-86231-3

ALL I WANT IS YOU

Copyright © 2011 by Sade Odubiyi

www.kimanipress.com

Printed in U.S.A.

Dear Reader,

Have you ever wanted to be someone else? Ever
wanted to live a different life and start all over again?
Monica Dupree does. Once an international icon
known as "Venus," she now hides her captivating
eyes behind sunglasses and her famous figure under
baggy clothes. After the death of her husband, Monica
has many secrets to hide. Secrets JD Rozan wants to
uncover.

I found it intriguing delving into Monica's life and the
reasons why she wanted to change. As a writer, change
is easy. With a few words I can change a sunny day to
one filled with thunderclouds. I can add forty pounds
to a character or make them as thin as a reed. But
one thing I've learned in writing is that change always
comes with a consequence.

And that's what happens when Monica and JD indulge
in a sexy fantasy. They learn that every choice has a
price....

Enjoy,

Dara Girard

Prologue

"She's gone."

The man behind the ornate desk didn't move and for a moment Reginald Bower wasn't sure he'd heard him. But that wasn't uncommon. Anton Stevens was a hard man to read. The unrelenting African sun had polished his smooth, dark skin to onyx. His striking features were unmarked by any blemishes or wrinkles, making his exact age a mystery. He could range from early thirties to mid-fifties. His slender face sported clear rimless glasses, meticulously shaped eyebrows and a long jaw. He came across like a professor, but he was much more powerful than that. He stared at Reginald with an unsettling gaze, as if he'd heard a dull weather report.

Reginald hesitated then cleared his throat, a river of sweat sliding down his back. The two large standing fans that blew, making a light whirling sound in the otherwise quiet office, didn't abate the stifling heat.

He was still getting used to the stark climate change from Wisconsin weather to that of Ghana. At times he still couldn't believe how much his life had changed, but that wasn't the issue now. As the silence stretched on, Reginald resisted the urge to shift from one foot to the other. He had to stand still and firm and show no fear. He repeated the message just to make sure he had been heard. "She's gone."

"I heard you the first time," Stevens said in a cool, clipped British accent that belied the fury in his gaze. "How did it happen?" He let his gaze fall and pushed a paper aside so that it was aligned with the edge of the desk. It was a casual motion that made Reginald's anxiety grow. His boss was a man who liked order and didn't take well to anything out of place.

Reginald racked his mind trying to think of all of the different ways he could have prevented her escape. The compound had interior security and an eight-foot iron gate. Beyond the gate they were still miles away from any city or town. How she'd been able to cross over fifty acres without being attacked by the wild animals that wandered onto the property, or consumed by the imminent threat of dehydration, confounded him. But he knew that if she was clever, she could feast on the lush grove of fruit trees. Reginald groaned. Perhaps he should have done another search before coming to Stevens, but it would have been a waste of time. He doubted she was out there, and he knew his second search wouldn't have reassured his boss.

Reginald had had the security guards search the nearest village, but no one had seen her. And she would be hard to miss. A six-foot beauty with cascading dark hair, legendary hazel eyes and light caramel skin would stand out.

He'd been in security for ten years now, and working for Stevens had been the highlight of his career. He had more money than he'd ever seen before, and now one woman had put his job in jeopardy. When he found her again, he would make her pay.

Reginald cleared his throat again, knowing that Stevens was waiting for a response. His boss was patient and wouldn't repeat himself. He was a dangerous man and Reginald knew it was best not to upset him, but he also knew there was no way to tell him the news without doing exactly that. *How did it happen?* God, he wished he knew. "Um…we're still figuring that out."

Stevens clasped his hands together. "I see."

A drop of sweat slid down Reginald's forehead, but he knew better than to wipe it away. "But we're looking—"

Stevens held up his hand. "I only gave you one job, and that was to look after one of my favorite possessions."

"Yes, sir."

"And you failed me."

"Sir—"

"Since you have carelessly lost what was mine, how do you plan to get it back for me?"

"We're on it right now, sir. We recently discovered that she's no longer in the country, and we are certain she'll hide with her family."

Stevens shook his head. "Don't be an idiot." He held up his hand. "Forget I said that. Evidently you already are, since you've let a woman escape a hundred-room compound, twenty acres inside the gates, fifty acres of surrounding property and at least a hundred miles to the nearest village, where she can easily slip into Togo or the Ivory Coast. She has connections all over the world and speaks three languages. So the fact that you know she's 'out of the country' means nothing to me. After her husband's death, she only has a sister living, and she wouldn't be careless enough to go to her."

"She's not in Africa."

"Really?"

"At least she won't be for long. She's going to the United States."

Stevens raised his eyebrows with surprise and interest. "How do you know that?"

"One of the girls mentioned that she felt safe there."

Stevens released a weary sigh and took out a small, red cloth. "You've put me in a very unfortunate position." He took off his glasses and cleaned a lens. "If she talks or says anything about me, that would cause trouble."

"I'm sure she won't. If she talks about you, that would lead us to her. Don't worry. We will find her."

"I'm sure you'll try." Stevens sighed with disappointment. "Are you married?"

"Yes."

"Children?"

"No, not yet."

Stevens nodded and replaced his glasses. "Good. Family is important." He gestured to the door. "You may go."

"Thank you, sir." Reginald turned, relieved that he'd

gotten off easy. He began walking to the door but never made it. He was dead before he hit the ground.

Anton put his revolver aside, pleased that he'd hit his target with minimal mess. It was too bad. He'd liked Reginald.

Anton hit the intercom on his desk phone. "Send a bouquet of flowers to Reginald Bower's widow. Then find Hicks. I have a job for him."

Anton disconnected then clasped his hands together and counted to ten. He had to remain calm. He swirled his chair around to stare out at the lush landscape. Years ago he had purchased nearly one hundred acres and had spent most of his life transforming it into an oasis, or at least that was what it was to him. The wide assortment of tropical flowers and several types of palm trees provided a brilliant burst of colors and a wide assortment of intoxicating smells. From childhood he had always shown an interest in botany and had cultivated a love for gardening. Not that he did the gardening directly. He never dirtied himself. He preferred to leave that task to the gardeners and biologists he had hired over the years.

Unfortunately, all was not paradise. He had failed in getting the extra twenty-five acres he wanted from an eccentric elderly Norwegian woman, who refused to sell her portion of land to him. He wasn't used to not getting what he wanted, but he was patient and knew that the frail woman wouldn't last very long.

Twice he'd had his prized possessions take refuge on her property, all without her knowledge, but they'd been captured and punished. None had tried again— until Venus.

Anton watched a bright green-and-yellow lizard dart past and sighed. How could she do this to him? He'd given her everything—shelter, clothes, jewels, the finest wines in the world—and she'd treated him like this? Anton balled his hands into fists.

"You're a little nobody and nothing!" his mother used to tell him, leaving him to the various nannies she hired while she and his father went to parties and traveled without him. But he'd shown her. Now he was a powerful man with women who adored him. No one would treat him like a nobody again. He wouldn't let them. He deserved better treatment, and he'd get it. He wouldn't let Venus upset him. She was just afraid. He hadn't handled her right, but once he found her, he would do better next time. She belonged to him. Such beauty couldn't be hidden for long. Someone would see her. His Venus would not escape him.

Anton stood then stopped when he spotted Reginald's body on the floor. He'd completely forgotten about it. It was Venus's fault for his actions. He knelt next to Reginald and pulled out his wallet. He flipped through it, stopping briefly at the picture of the man's wife. The image surprised him. He didn't know people still carried around photographs of loved ones anymore. Pity. He must have really loved her, but he doubted it would have lasted. Women were deceivers and heartbreakers; he'd done him a favor. He sighed then patted Reginald on the back. "So Venus is heading to the States. It seems you're going to help me find my Venus after all."

Chapter 1

On a clear summer afternoon, two intruders entered Monica Dupree's life. She was forced to kill the first one, but she knew the second one was far more dangerous. She set her rifle on her shoulder, trying to portray a calm she didn't feel. Her heart continued to hammer in her chest while the sound of the fired shot echoed in her ears. All around her was still, as though a photographer had captured the scene in a picture. The clearing in the woods suddenly felt too silent—no birds sang, no creatures scurried past, not even the wind dared to blow. Nothing moved. Her gaze fell on the lifeless dog that only seconds ago had been a snarling, vicious beast out for blood.

"Thank you," a deep voice said, yanking her out of her thoughts.

Monica abruptly turned her attention to the man whose life she'd probably saved. He leaned against a tree with one arm held at an angle. Monica fought back a frown. She didn't want his "thanks." She didn't want him here. She wanted him to be somewhere else far away from this town and this property. Solomon Island wasn't really a complete island, but it was given the name because a large part of its eastern and southern land mass was separated from the main state of Georgia by a river. It boasted numerous independent farmlands, some working and others merely vanity, and its location near the water invited an influx of tourists, especially during the summer months.

For nearly a year Monica had thought of this land and farmhouse as her own. Her seventy-five-year-old landlady lived in town with a friend and had rented the entire property to her because she thought the house had gotten too big for her and she wanted someone to look after it. It was no longer a working farm, and it hadn't been so in decades, but there was still plenty to manage. Monica had thought of it as her private sanctuary after her husband's passing. A place of safety. The past ten months had been heavenly, her own Eden, and now a snake was in her midst.

No, that wasn't fair, Monica quickly corrected herself. She hardly knew the man, but she'd planned to live there alone for the rest of her life. Unfortunately, Nadine Rozan, her landlady, had forced her to alter her plans. She'd said her grandson was coming to the farm for rest and relaxation. So she and her grandson would be sharing the large house for the next several weeks. Roommates. The last thing Monica wanted was a roommate, especially a male one.

Fortunately, the five-bedroom house was spacious

enough that she probably would rarely see him. Besides, she spent most of her time in her studio or going for long walks. She didn't need to worry. She was safe. Anton couldn't find her. It had been eleven months, four days, eight hours, seven minutes and ten seconds since she'd escaped him. She'd been careful to make sure to leave her trail cold. She planned never to resurface to her old life.

Monica sighed. That still didn't make having to deal with some overworked businessman any easier.

"You're going to love him, dear," Nadine had said a week earlier as the two women cleaned up one of the extra rooms. It was located directly across from Monica's bedroom, but Nadine had insisted. "All the women do. They can't help it. Once you see him, you'll know why."

Monica plastered on a grin to be polite. She knew that no matter how charming or handsome Nadine's grandson was, he'd have no effect on her. She'd been around men like him all her life—handsome men, rich men, powerful men. She'd married one who was a combination of all three, and now she was alone. She was fine with that. Ready to be her own woman, something she'd never had a chance to be before.

"He won't get in your way," Nadine continued. "Just make sure he doesn't work too much."

"I'm sure he'll be fine," Monica said, in no mood to be stuck babysitting a grown man.

Nadine hesitated, sending Monica a scrutinizing gaze. "It wouldn't hurt you to get a nice dress to meet him."

"Why?" Monica said with a laugh. "Does he need a welcome committee?"

"A pretty face is always a nice welcome."

"I'm not buying a brand-new dress or changing my hair or putting on makeup for anyone. I'm happy the way I am. There are plenty of women in town if he wants a summer fling."

"But you shouldn't hide yourself away the way you do," Nadine said, unwilling to let the topic drop. "I'm sure you could be a pretty girl if you tried."

"Maybe," Monica said in a noncommittal tone. "Now let's get his room in order." Monica suppressed the urge to laugh. She'd never been called pretty before. She'd always been seen as something more. From the age of four, she remembered the looks and stares from strangers. The way her parents kept her close, as if afraid someone would steal her away.

"What an extraordinary child."

"Have you ever seen such eyes, and that dark hair is gorgeous."

"You could make millions on that face."

"What an absolute beauty."

"Go on, Venus, use that smile. Every woman will want to go out and buy this lipstick."

"You're a goddess, Venus! No man can resist."

"Work it, Venus, work it!"

But those days were gone. Monica wasn't a vision or an expression of someone else's ideal anymore. She was just an ordinary woman, and that was a privilege she didn't plan on giving up.

Monica quickly sized up the man in front of her. He met her expectations. He wore a tailored dark suit, as if he'd arrived at the Ritz-Carlton for a board meeting instead of a farmhouse for a holiday. He was tall. Few men were taller than she was, but he beat her by several inches. He carried himself well and had clean-cut features that were a little harsh but not off-putting, and sharp assessing eyes. His mouth was a problem, however. It was fuller than she'd imagined. His dark lashes and broad brows softened his features, hinting at both a vulnerability and gentleness she didn't want to see.

Even if she hadn't sworn off men, Monica knew he wasn't her type.

Her husband had been fun and daring. No two days were the same. He could... Monica bit her lip. No, she wouldn't think about him. It was still too painful. Everything would have been different if he'd listened to her. She didn't blame him for dying. She blamed him for living so recklessly, for ignoring her pleas to stop car racing, to stop mountain climbing and taking numerous other risks. But she knew he wouldn't have felt alive if he'd given up those activities. During his last moments, Monica knew he'd felt free. And he ended his life on his terms.

He'd performed his last stunt to celebrate a grand gallery showing called "Living Large." A camera crew was on hand to witness his every move. It was a stunt he'd performed many times before—scaling down a zip line from a large office building to the entrance of another. The act had become his signature performance. But he'd descended too fast and collided with the building at approximately a hundred miles an hour. Some said his reflexes had been too slow, others that he'd rigged the gears himself because of a cancer scare.

Monica was the only one who knew there had been another reason.

Monica angrily pushed the thought aside. She wouldn't let herself ever be that hurt again. Yep, JD Rozan met her expectations. What she didn't expect was the puppy cradled in his arms. The one he'd valiantly protected from the other dog's violent attack. That protective instinct surprised her, because it seemed to contradict the hard image he portrayed.

"I don't need you to thank me," she said in a sharp voice. "You must be JD."

He held out his free hand. "Yes, JD Rozan."

She quickly shook it. "Monica Dulane," she said, careful to use her alias. "You need to be careful. You can't just wander around out here."

Her sharp tone didn't seem to faze him. His gaze scanned the area, a wistful look on his face. "I used to walk around out here when I was a kid."

"Things have changed," she said in a flat tone.

JD's sharp gaze returned to her face. "I can see that," he said, motioning to her rifle. "But I heard this little guy whimpering—" he looked down at the puppy "—and followed the sound here. I found him tied up to a tree stump by his hind legs. I'd just untied him when that one showed up." He gestured to the second dog lying still off to the side.

Monica walked over to the dead dog and shook her head. It was a shame. He'd been trained to kill. It wasn't his fault. She'd have to bury him. She didn't want to attract scavengers. All she needed was a gang of vultures making this spot their new home. She looked at the dead dog again, measuring its size, then noticed a mark on its paw. She swore.

"What?" JD asked.

"This is one of Drent Marks's dogs." Monica looked around and saw more evidence of Drent's presence: the torn tree bark where various ropes had been tied, the flattened ground, and the trash and blood on dry leaves.

JD watched her. "What do you see?"

"There have been dogfights here. They used to have them in the shed before I stopped them. I'll talk to Drent later. He's the ringleader. That's another reason to be careful out here. Some people started squatting on your grandmother's property bringing with them bad behavior. It took me four months to get them off, but it's not easy and, as you can see, some people don't listen."

"Now that I'm here, I'll handle any trouble."

Monica didn't believe him. He was going to be there only about eight weeks. She didn't expect him to be able to accomplish much, so she decided not to reply. "Did he get you?" she asked, noticing JD's torn sleeve.

JD glanced down at his ripped jacket sleeve. "Nearly, but not quite."

Monica nodded. "He wasn't focused on you. He was trying to get to him," she said, gesturing to the puppy, which didn't move. If she hadn't know it was real, she would have thought it was a toy—its large eyes terrified and unblinking.

JD frowned. "Bait?" he asked, looking down at the helpless animal.

Monica did the same, and from the many scars covering its head and face, she knew that in its short life the little fellow had been attacked many times before.

"Yes, probably," she said with disgust. "That's how Drent likes to train his monsters."

"Then Drent and I will have a little chat."

Monica looked at JD, startled by the aggressive tone in his voice. "He's not someone to antagonize."

JD flashed a grin as cold as a lethal blade. "Neither am I."

Monica felt a chill go through her and decided to change the subject. "You're early. I didn't expect you for another two days."

JD shrugged without apology. "I just had to get away."

He didn't expand on his answer and Monica didn't try to push him. She wasn't really interested in why he was here. She had to deal with the situation as best she could. "Okay, let's go inside."

JD took the rifle from her and handed the puppy to her before she could protest.

"If this Marks guy shows up," he said with purpose, "I want to be ready."

Chapter 2

Marks didn't show up and they made it to the house without incident. Once inside they went to the kitchen and focused on the still-paralyzed puppy.

"I don't know where the bleeding is coming from," JD said, running his fingers through the puppy's coarse fur.

He bent toward Monica as she held the puppy, and she felt her pulse quicken. He smelled like aftershave, fresh leaves and a scent all his own—a heady mix that reminded her of sleek luxury cars, lemon martinis and exotic cities. Their faces nearly met, but he didn't seem to notice because he was so intent on his task. Monica took the opportunity to study his face some more—his skin was smooth like chestnuts, and that sensuous bottom lip was distracting. She felt her face grow warm. She dropped her gaze to his hand and froze.

"Wait a minute." She grabbed his hand. "It's you."

She turned his hand over and noticed the dried and fresh blood on his wrist and palm.

Monica set the frightened puppy on the counter, but not before grabbing a dish towel to make a makeshift bed. "You lied to me."

JD shook his head. "I didn't lie."

"You told me that he didn't get you," she said, taking off his jacket.

"He didn't."

Monica rested JD's bloodied jacket over a kitchen stool nearby then rolled up his sleeve and saw the wound. "Really? Then what do you call this?"

JD sighed, resigned. "I didn't get that from the puppy."

Monica walked over to the sink and grabbed a fresh dish rag hanging on a hook. She put it under the running water, wrung the excess water out and began cleaning what appeared to be a large gash. She narrowed her eyes. "It looks like a knife wound." Monica raised her gaze to his, surprised. "What happened? Were you stabbed?"

JD rubbed his forehead then let his hand fall. "It was an accident." He reached for the rag. "Here, let me do that."

Monica pushed his hand away. "You can't accidentally do this to someone."

"Then call it a misunderstanding."

Monica searched his face and spotted a brief look of embarrassment. She began to grin. "A misunderstanding?"

"Yes," JD said in a tight voice.

Her grin grew. "You don't seem the type to get into bar brawls, so it must be a woman."

"The bandage must have come off in the woods," he said, trying to make light of the situation. "I'll re-bandage it later." He began to roll down his sleeve.

Monica stopped him. "No, we'll do it now."

JD stilled, suddenly making her aware of how close they were, how warm his skin felt and how small her hand looked as she covered his. He had large, strong hands. He could fight her—and win—if he wanted to.

"You're used to getting your way, aren't you?" he said.

Monica snatched her hand away and kept her tone neutral. "The last thing I need is for you to get an infection and get sick. Your grandmother would blame me for not looking after you." Monica studied the cut, desperate to look at something else besides his face and clever brown eyes. "But you're right, she—whoever she was—didn't mean to kill you. Either that or you just got out of the way fast enough, because you don't need stitches, thank goodness. I'll get my first aid kit. You might as well take off your shirt. It's ruined anyway. It's torn and has blood on it."

"I think my trousers are torn, too."

Monica paused. His face was serious, but his tone sounded playful. Was he flirting with her? No, that couldn't be. Men never flirted with her anymore. "I don't care if they are," she said in a prim voice that belied her pounding heart. At that moment, she pictured him standing naked in the kitchen as the afternoon sun skimmed over every inch of his beautiful body. "You can keep those on."

"If you say so," JD said as she left the kitchen. Monica went into the bathroom and grabbed the kit from under the sink. She straightened then stared at her reflection in the mirror. "What is wrong with you?" she scolded herself. "Get your act together. Your mind is playing tricks on you. How could he be flirting with that?" She looked at the dowdy-looking woman with big, tinted sunglasses gazing back at her. She'd worked hard to perfect her new image as Monica Dulane. Few people knew her maiden name was Dupree, but she didn't want to take the risk of using it. However, she also didn't want a name she wouldn't easily adjust to, so she kept her first name and just altered the second.

Although her new name was similar to her old one, her new look was the exact opposite of her former appearance. She'd perfected an eccentric bohemian look by wearing free-flowing dresses in dull browns and greens and kept her luxurious, long black hair covered in an assortment of printed head wraps. All that she had done to hide her identity had been successful, but her greatest disguise was her stylish, wraparound sunglasses, which made her look as if she was stuck back in the seventies.

Monica had come up with a very believable story that explained why she always had to wear them. She had told Nadine, and anyone who asked, that she'd been born with a congenital eye disease that affected her retina and made her eyes extremely sensitive to light. As a result, she had to wear special glasses all the time, even indoors, to protect them. At first Nadine hadn't been convinced and thought Monica must be legally blind because the tint on the glasses made it impossible to see her eyes, but she soon got used to it.

The thick frame covered just above her eyebrows to the middle of her cheek, obscuring one of her most attractive features—her prominent cheekbones. The industry had defined her as having one of the most stunning profiles. That profile was now gone.

Monica shook her head at her reflection. No, he hadn't been flirting, just teasing. It had all been her imagination. She had been without male attention too long.

Monica took a deep, fortifying breath then returned to the kitchen. She found JD sitting at the kitchen island with his shirt off, scratching the puppy under its chin. He certainly wasn't built like a man who spent hours behind a desk. He looked tough, hard and powerful. He was all sinewy muscle without a soft spot on him.

"I can't get him to relax," JD said, snapping Monica out of her wayward thoughts.

Monica shifted her gaze and noticed that the puppy's eyes were closed. "He likes what you're doing."

JD's eyes met hers as if they shared an intimate secret, and for a second it felt as if he could see past the shield of her lens. "Then I'll keep doing it."

She lowered her eyes, determined to focus on the matter at hand. She opened the kit, twisted off the top of a bottle of antiseptic ointment and dabbed it on a cotton ball. "Now this might sting."

"No problem. I—" JD bit back a curse word when she applied the medication then gripped his hand into a fist. "What the hell is that? Acid?"

Monica tried not to laugh. "It will keep the wound clean."

"Getting stabbed hurt less than that."

"You're making it sound worse than it is."

His eyes twinkled. "Probably."

Monica swallowed, liking the sight of his eyes more than she wanted to. She quickly wrapped the bandage. "There. All done."

"Thank you again. Now I owe you two favors."

She restocked the kit. "I'm not keeping track."

JD picked up and replaced a box of Band-Aids, his hand lightly brushing hers, his voice low with promise. "I am."

Monica felt her face grow warm again. This was ridiculous. She never blushed. Well, Venus didn't. Obviously, Monica did.

"Do you think he's hungry?" JD asked, scratching the puppy behind the ears.

"I may have some scraps to hold him until he can get some proper dog food."

"Good. We'll give him a good meal before we get him checked out."

Monica was surprised by how quickly JD used the word "we," but she didn't feel like correcting him. She reached up and grabbed a small bowl from a cabinet and went to the fridge to get some leftover food. She took a glass container and set it on the table. Monica pried open the container and was about to pour its contents out when JD shook his head. "No, don't feed him that."

She looked at him, surprised. "Why not?"

"It looks too good."

She replaced the top and grabbed another dish. When she opened it, JD shook his head again.

"What now?"

"These are gourmet meals. Ravioli, Swedish meatballs. You can't feed food like that to a dog."

"Sure I can. I made them."

"You cooked these?"

"I don't have a chef on hand," Monica said with a note of sarcasm.

JD selected the ravioli and handed the bowl to her. "Could you heat that up for me? I didn't have lunch and your food would be like manna from the gods." His gaze traveled lazily over her face, as if he was a sugar addict studying a powdered doughnut. She could no longer deny it. He was definitely flirting. But why? Was it a natural habit of his to flirt with any woman he was with? That had to be it. There was no other reason a man like him would be interested. Monica opened her mouth to tell him that he could heat up his own food, but he continued before she could say anything. "I'll find something simple to feed Baxter."

Monica went over to the microwave. "Baxter?"

"You don't like the name?"

She set the timer. "No, it's fine."

JD grabbed the remainder of a turkey meat loaf, mashed the contents and put it in a bowl then set it and Baxter on the ground. "There you go."

Baxter sniffed the food then began to eat.

"He certainly has an appetite," JD said.

"I hope you didn't give him too much. I wouldn't want him to be sick."

"I didn't."

The buzzer on the microwave went off and Monica handed JD the dish and a plate.

"I don't need a plate," he said. "Just a fork."

"You can finish that?" she asked, setting a fork down on the counter so that he couldn't touch her again.

"Sure. If it tastes as good as it smells, I'll have no problem." JD took a bite then rested a hand over his heart. "Hmm...delicious."

"Thank you," she said, wishing he'd put his shirt back on. He had beautiful nipples—perfect and symmetrical. She wondered if he ever considered piercing one. A friend of Delong's had used a gold hoop with... *Stop it!* she scolded herself to repress memories that involved her deceased husband. She shouldn't have these thoughts. She couldn't.

"You cook all this just for yourself?"

Monica pinched herself hard then busied herself putting the plate away. "Yes, I like to cook. I find it relaxing. I cook a lot on the weekends so that in the week I can focus on my work and not have to worry about what to eat."

Cooking was a hobby she'd never been allowed to have before. As a working model, she had to keep her figure. She had to watch every bite she ate. Now she was free and had gained fifteen pounds and didn't mind a bit. Besides, there was no one to impress.

JD licked his lower lip, his pink tongue moistening it and making it more prominent. "I'll pay you."

She blinked. "What?"

"Whatever the groceries are, I'll pay just to enjoy a meal like this."

Monica dismissed his praise. "This was just an experiment."

"If they come out like this, then experiment away. You could start your own company. The tourist market is thriving here. Give them a quick, simple way to add an exotic twist to their meals, and they'd eat it up. You could—" He stopped and swore. "Sorry. It's a habit."

"Thinking business?"

"Yes," he said, his dark eyes studying her with acute interest. "And drawing out talent."

Monica shifted, feeling awkward under his gaze. "Well, from what your grandmother told me, you're here to take a break."

JD leaned back, his gaze never leaving her face. "What else did she tell you about me?"

Monica shrugged. "Nothing much. Just that you work hard and that she worries about you." She sent a significant look to his bandaged arm. "Considering the trouble you've already gotten into, I'm not surprised."

JD lifted a sly brow. "Fortunately, I know how to get myself out of trouble."

Monica folded her arms. "But trouble won't be following you here, will it?"

"No. I left it back in the city."

"I bet trouble has a name."

He flashed a quick grin. "I like to call her several names, but you won't have to worry about her or anyone else."

"Hmm," she said, doubtful.

"I have to give Gran a call. I plan to take her to the movies sometime soon." He set his fork down and stood. "Let me just get changed then we can go into town."

"We?" Monica said, her voice cracking with surprise. "Why?" she asked, following him out of the kitchen.

"To take this guy to the vet."

"But I don't need to go with you."

JD walked briskly to his car. "You look like you could use a drive, and things might have changed so much that I'd get lost." He opened up the trunk and reached for his suitcase. "It won't take long and—son of a…" He dropped the suitcase on the ground and swore.

Monica rushed toward him. "Are you all right?"

"I'm fine," he said through clenched teeth. He took a deep breath. "I just grabbed it with the wrong arm."

"I can take it for you." She reached down to lift it.

JD gently shoved her aside. "I'm an idiot, not an invalid." He walked back into the house then up the stairs. "Which room is mine?"

Monica hurried after him. "It's on the right, but—"

He opened the door, stopped in the doorway and looked around. *Watch his face,* she remembered Nadine had said, but Monica couldn't tell what he thought of the room. She didn't know what Nadine expected her to see. What would a man like JD think of a room with a strange mix of Midwestern wood furniture and a hand-carved bamboo side table. An enormous mahogany sleigh bed filled the room, accented by an elegant brass regency table lamp. Off to the side stood a handsome antique rolltop desk and an overstuffed leather executive chair. Behind it was a large window that framed the view outside like a work of art. Except for an abstract painting of a musician that hung over his bed, nothing else was displayed. Several tufted rugs added a needed warmth to the room, providing cover for the worn wooden floors.

"I got the larger room," Monica said to fill the silence. "But your grandmother made sure this one would be comfortable for you."

JD turned to her, but she still couldn't read his expression. "It's perfect," he said, but she didn't believe him. She was certain that he found something unsettling but sensed he wouldn't tell her what it was.

"If you need anything—"

"I won't be long." He winked. "Wait for me," he said then closed the door.

Monica stared at the door, stunned. He was like a steamroller. Stopping him was impossible, but she didn't have to go with him into town. His excuse to have her go with him was flimsy and ridiculous. He'd never get lost. She was sure his luxury car had a GPS system with a sexy female voice that would take him wherever he wanted to go.

Yes, she could refuse him. She *would* refuse him. The moment he came out of his bedroom she would tell him she wasn't going. She'd tell him that she had better things to do than chauffer him around. He probably thought she was a pushover, but she'd let him know different and she'd let him know now. Monica raised her hand to pound on the door at the same time JD opened it. She ended up hitting him in the chest.

She yanked her hand back. "Oh, sorry."

JD glanced down at the spot where she'd struck him, and the corner of his mouth kicked up in a quick grin. "No problem." His eyes met hers. "Told you I'd be quick." He was dressed in a pair of khaki trousers and a long-sleeve, cotton gray shirt. But the fact that his chest was now covered didn't seem to hamper her imagination. The shirt fit him well and the steel color seemed to symbolize his hard physique and manner.

But Monica wouldn't let him bully her. She had a resolve just as steely as his. "Yes, you did say that, but—"

JD brushed past her, his body pressing against hers before he went to the stairs. The moment was brief but not brief enough. For one wild instant his chest and those firm nipples of his touched her breasts like a caress. She knew that while he was here the farmhouse wouldn't be a place of safety. "Whatever you want to say, tell me on the road."

"That's just it," Monica said, trying to keep up with him as he bounded down the stairs. "I don't need to take you."

JD scooped up Baxter, who'd remained curled up in a rumpled blanket, and grabbed a set of keys. "You're right. I don't need you to." He tossed her the keys. "You're driving," he said and headed for the front door.

"But you just said you don't need—"

He abruptly stopped and turned to face her.

Monica stumbled back before she crashed into him.

"I don't need a lot of things," he said. "I want you to come with me. It's as simple as that."

Monica blinked and her mouth suddenly felt dry. "Why?"

"I like your company." He opened the front door and left.

For the second time that day Monica stood stunned.

He liked her company? Perhaps she was just a one-day novelty for him. He probably needed a change from the type of people who were willing to stab him to make a point. Perhaps a quick drive wouldn't be much trouble, and she wanted to see what the vet had to say about the puppy. Afterward they'd go back to doing their own things. Monica turned and locked the door, feeling more in control.

Perhaps the more time she spent with him, the sooner her heart would get back to normal.

Chapter 3

She fascinated him. JD knew it was rude to stare, but he couldn't help himself. He found Monica Dulane intriguing. Her head was wrapped in a brown scarf with abstract shapes in black and white, but he saw a hint of coal-black hair which gave her the appearance of a cloistered nun; her glasses, with heavily tinted lenses, were too big for her face, and her clothes draped her like a sack, their colors as exciting as dry leaves. He found her dusty skin and a glimpse of her high cheekbones alluring, and noticed that she carried herself with an elegance that contradicted her dowdy outer appearance. She didn't look more than thirty, but she dressed as if she were two decades older. He'd never forget the sight of her with a rifle in her hand or the feel of her soft, slender fingers against his skin as she bandaged his wound.

The thought of his wound made JD inwardly groan.

He'd have to deal with *that* situation later. He glanced in the rearview mirror at Baxter sleeping on a pile of towels in the backseat. At least he wasn't too much of a complication. JD already had enough to deal with. He returned his gaze to the mysterious woman in the driver's seat. She sat erect and each motion was efficient—a confident, capable woman who he was certain wasn't all that she seemed.

Monica touched her cheek. "Is there something on my face?"

"No. I was just wondering what a young woman like you is doing hiding out here."

"I'm not that young and I'm not hiding. I like my life."

JD looked out at the two-lane country road, expansive woods and the farmland that bordered it. "But nothing happens here."

"That's what I like."

"Recovering from a divorce?"

"No, I've never married," she said.

JD nodded, not surprised. "Where were you before you came here?"

"I traveled."

"Doing what?" he pressed, not satisfied with her vague answer.

Monica tapped her thumb against the steering wheel. "I was an assistant to a top fashion model, but I can't tell you her name."

"Right." JD tilted his head to the side and studied her profile. "And you didn't get any tips from her?"

Monica furrowed her brow. "Tips?"

"Yes," he said with a broad sweep of his hand. "About clothes and makeup and that stuff."

"As long as she looked good and I made her life work, it didn't matter what *I* looked like."

"Being around glamorous people didn't rub off on you?" JD asked, amazed. "That takes a strong character."

"I don't need to be glamorous. I like how I look. My clothes are comfortable and my glasses work. If you don't like it, you can just ignore me."

JD let his eyes trail down her dress then up again.

Monica gripped the steering wheel. "You're still staring."

"I know."

"It's rude."

"Just tell me what you're hiding from and I'll stop."

Monica gripped the steering wheel until her knuckles paled. "I told you. I'm not hiding from anything or anyone. Just because a woman doesn't dress to attract men, she's suddenly all sorts of things—stuck-up, prudish, a wallflower, an ex-convict."

JD laughed. "An ex-convict? Really?"

"Yes," she said without humor. "This town is very inventive when it comes to rumors." Monica relaxed her grip a fraction. "Besides, when you're ready to tell me the real reason for your stab wound and why you decided to wander into the woods instead of coming into the house then I'll tell you more about myself. Until then it's none of your business."

"Fair enough." He held up a hand as if making a pledge. "No more personal questions."

"Thank you."

"But I still want to see it."

Monica turned to him, alarmed. "See what?"

Her surprise made him burst into laughter. "What do you think I'm talking about?"

"I don't know."

"Well, it's nothing that personal, if that's what's bothering you."

"Nothing is bothering me," Monica said in a curt tone. "I just didn't expect the question. What do you want to see?"

JD lowered his voice and his gaze slid down her dress. "What are you willing to show me?"

Monica stared at him, openmouthed. "You are the most aggravating male—"

"I want to see your studio," he interrupted with a grin. "My grandmother told me you have one. What do you do?"

Monica shook her head. "I don't believe this."

"What? It's not a personal question. You know I'm in business."

"You're not in business—you *are* business. You've created six companies, two of which you sold for millions, and stopped the investment firm, Davidson & Daniels, from being swallowed up in a hostile takeover. You were also instrumental in helping the Securities and Exchange Commission bring down investor Glen Niel for fraud."

His eyes lit up with pleasure. "Ah, so you've been reading up on me?"

"Your grandmother likes to brag."

"Okay, then it's only fair that I know a little more about you."

Monica sighed, resigned. "I create jewelry."

"For people?"

She turned to him, confused. "Who else?"

"In some circles you'd be surprised what people buy their babies and pets." JD playfully tugged on her ear. "How come you don't wear any?"

She swatted his hand away. "I just don't."

"Why not? Or is that a personal question?"

It was personal. She couldn't say *I don't wear jewelry because I used to be cased in it. Diamonds and rubies. Emeralds and sapphires. People would flock to see the latest fashion I wore and I was a constant advertisement for somebody's product, which I don't want to be anymore.*

"It's just not a preference."

JD toyed with her earlobe again, this time looking closely. "You must wear them sometimes because your ears are pierced."

Monica pushed his hand away again. "Weren't you taught to keep your hands to yourself?"

"Yes, but I've never had a woman complain before."

"Touch me again and I'll bite you."

"Hmm," he said in a deep voice. "That might be fun."

"Fun?"

"Yes, to have my hand in your mouth."

Monica glared at him. "You are—"

JD grabbed her chin and turned her face forward. "Watch the road. You wouldn't want us to crash."

Monica gritted her teeth and glared at the road. He wasn't flirting with her. He was making fun of her— secretly laughing at her clothes and way of life. For a moment she wanted to rip off her disguise and let him see who he was really messing with. With one look she knew she could turn his knees into putty and remove that arrogant gleam from his eyes. But he didn't matter. Let him think he was having a little harmless fun with a backwoods nobody who appeared to be shy of men.

JD shifted in his seat to study her more. "So how did you get started? Do you have a plan? Who are your distributors?"

"You're sounding like a businessman again."

"Probably because I am."

"You're supposed to be on vacation."

He sighed. "Just tell me it's profitable and I'll leave you alone."

"It's profitable."

"Are you saying that because it's true or because you want me to leave you alone?"

Monica grinned. "Take a wild guess."

"I might be able to help you."

"I don't need your help."

JD held up his hands in surrender. "Okay, I won't talk business, but I'd still like to see your studio. I've always been fascinated by how the artistic mind works."

"If you're expecting chaos and drugs, you'll be disappointed. I'm very ordinary."

He tilted his head to the side. "One thing I don't think you are is ordinary."

Gerald Hicks set his phone down on his side table and grinned. He was back in action. Boy, did he like the runners. The ones who ran away from their handlers made life exciting. Hunting them down always kept him in top condition. Finding them exercised a muscle he needed to keep fit. He couldn't afford to get rusty. He had to get into the runner's life. He had to learn her (it was always a female) psyche. Delve into her childhood. Uncover family and friends then assimilate into their lives. Before long he knew how to think like them and anticipate their every move. Technology had helped him in his business, but he also liked going out in the field. He liked being a free agent.

He'd started out as a bounty hunter, but the job wasn't as glamorous and well paying as he'd hoped, so he decided to switch sides. He quickly learned that criminals paid much better and they didn't care about which methods he used. Not that he ever hurt a woman, but in order to find them he had to be morally flexible. He worked by referrals only; his reputation was his calling card. But he'd never had to handle a runaway from Stevens before. He usually kept his property in line. The guy must be slipping. But work had been slow lately and he was in the mood to travel, and the fee to work for Stevens could afford him that bit of luxury.

It would be the first time he'd searched for a goddess. He was ready to start. He swung his legs over the side of the bed.

"You're leaving now?" the woman lying in the bed beside him asked in a sleepy tone.

Anika always kept his bed warm between jobs. She was a simple woman and that's what he needed. "I've got work to do."

"Another assignment?"

"Yep."

She trailed one long, manicured red nail down his arm. "Baby, they work you too hard."

He laughed. She was an expensive hobby—if he didn't work he wouldn't be able to keep her. "I like my work."

"How long will you be this time?"

"Depends."

"On what?"

Venus. A woman who'd outsmarted one of the best. "My target."

"Except for the scratches he's in good condition," Dr. Treena Ikes, the veterinarian, said after a quick assessment of Baxter. She was an attractive woman with cornrows and a fresh face that made one think of mint julep and sunflowers. "He's a little underweight, but with a few meals that can be remedied. I'm glad you brought him to see me."

JD shook his head, amazed. "I can't believe you're still here. When they said Dr. Ikes, I was expecting your father."

"He retired years ago."

"And you decided to take over?"

"Yes. I was never just a weekender like you. I've always lived in this town. It's home and I have no reason to leave." She winked. "Unless you plan to give me one."

Treena was right. Although his grandparents had bought the property over fifty years ago, because it hadn't been their main residence the Rozans were considered weekenders. JD had been mostly a summer boy. He'd spent his time there during those holiday months, but after his father's death those visits became more infrequent then after high school almost nonexistent. He'd zip in for a quick visit, but he never stayed more than a week. Over the years his grandmother had scolded him and urged him to visit more often and longer, but he'd always come up with a reason not to.

But not this time. This time her invitation sounded like heaven. JD glanced at the wedding ring on her finger. "I heard you married William. Wouldn't he mind?"

Treena laughed. "Pay him enough and he wouldn't."

"You don't mean that."

She sighed and sobered. "No, not really, but things have been tight and that always strains things. It's his business, you see. He owns the general store next door and it's starting to lose money."

"I could talk to him. I know a little something about business."

Treena smiled. "You don't have to be modest, JD. Everyone knows how good you are at it."

"Just give me his card and—"

Treena hesitated. "He's a proud man. You'll have to tread carefully."

"I'll do my best, but if he's not willing to listen, there's not much I can do."

Treena wrote down her husband's number then handed it to JD. "Thanks."

"Save it. I haven't done anything yet." He stood. "So I can just leave Baxter in the shelter then?"

Treena sighed. "No."

"What?"

"He's all cleaned up, but that won't help him." She looked at the puppy with pity. "Poor thing."

"What do you mean? Is something else wrong with him?"

"The biggest strike against him is that Drent Marks once owned him. Because of that they'll put him down."

"But you just said he was healthy."

"Yes, physically, but psychologically..." She released a heavy sigh. "In order to have any chance of being adopted, he'd have to be fostered. We don't have anyone to foster him right now, and as skittish as he is it will be hard to place him, even if someone is willing to overlook all those vicious cuts and bite marks on his face." She stared at the dog on the table. "I mean, he's less than two years old, yet he doesn't move, he doesn't sniff the air or move around to explore. He's terrified and frozen. It will take patience to get him to become a normal dog again."

JD shrugged. "I can do it. I'll foster him for you."

"You?" she said, stunned. "You've never even owned goldfish."

"True, but my Gran used to own animals and I'd help out anytime I came to visit. You know that. That's how we first met, when her German shepherd broke its leg. She also had a horse, a rabbit and a few chickens."

"Yes, I remember." Treena grinned. "I also remember I had the biggest crush on you and you never even noticed me."

"I noticed you."

"You did?"

"But William noticed you first."

Treena dramatically rolled her eyes. "It would have been nice if you'd at least put up a fight."

"I would have lost anyway."

Treena laughed. "Maybe."

"So it's settled. I'll foster Baxter."

Treena hesitated. "I'm not sure you'd—"

"I'm here for a few weeks and I could get him used to a home environment. Then when I leave I'll drop him back here."

"He's going to take a lot of patience."

"That's something I have in spades."

"He might get attached to you."

"He won't."

"You sound sure."

"I am. People or things just don't get attached to me and I don't get attached to them."

Treena studied JD for a moment then picked up the puppy and handed it to him. "I heard *she* brought you in."

"She?"

"Yes, the woman renting your grandmother's place."

"Oh, right, Monica."

"What's her story? The moment I saw her in the waiting lounge I nearly fainted. She's like a ghost. People rarely see her outside the farmhouse. She keeps it neat but you never see her mowing the lawn or trimming the bushes. Some think she does it at night because of her eyes. And she hardly comes into town. When she does, she doesn't talk to anyone. Just keeps to herself. How did you get her to come out here?"

"I used my charm."

"I'm sorry I asked."

"No you're not. You know I have a way with women."

Treena patted JD playfully on the cheek. "Which means you know about as much about her as I do."

"I plan to find out more. I've never seen a woman handle a rifle the way she did."

"A rifle?"

JD briefly told Treena about the incident in the woods. Treena gave a low whistle. "She killed one of Drent's dogs? She is brave."

"She's a lot more than that."

Treena stared at him and widened her eyes. "Don't tell me you're interested in her."

"I've always liked a mystery."

"Dressed like a sack of potatoes?" Treena said with a sniff. "She's more skittish than that dog. She's definitely not your type."

"True. But that doesn't mean I'm not curious."

Treena opened the door and shook her head. "You always were addicted to trouble."

"Challenges," JD corrected.

"Remember when you climbed Mrs. Vanooth's huge oak tree to rescue her cat, and it scratched you and you lost your balance and fell?"

"I remember."

"You broke your wrist and two ribs."

"I'm older now."

"Maybe," she said, patting JD on the back. "But this one has bigger claws."

Monica frowned when she saw JD with the puppy. "What's wrong with him?"

"They need him to be fostered, so I volunteered."

"To do what?"

"Foster him." When she continued to look blank he added, "I'm taking him home."

"Are you kidding me?"

"Why would I be kidding you?"

Monica waved her hands in a helpless gesture, searching for words. "It's just…you don't seem the type to have the patience."

"Then you don't know me very well. I can be very patient if something matters to me. This little guy needs a break, and the first thing I need to do is pick up a few things."

They went to the general store next door, which allowed pets, and bought a fluffy dog bed, a water and food dish and wet and dry dog food.

JD looked up and saw Treena's husband come out from the back and waved at him. "Hey, Hostie," he said, using William's last name, "I just came from seeing Treena. You're a lucky man."

William sent him a bored look. He was a lean man with a trim beard. "I know," he replied in a flat voice.

JD lowered his voice. "She told me that things have been a little slow. I'd like to talk—"

"I don't need to talk," William interrupted as he moved away. "Business is fine."

JD looked around the almost empty store. Except for himself, Monica and Baxter, there were only two other customers, yet outside the sidewalk bustled with people. "But it sounds like it could always be better. I could—"

"You could mind your own business. You haven't

changed. You and your family always thinking you know more and are better than everyone else just 'cause you had a second home and could leave whenever you liked."

"That's not—"

"Why the hell are you back here? Everyone wants to know. Your grandmother's place had been sitting nearly empty for years being maintained by the Wooley brothers until she suddenly decides to move out and rent it out for no reason," he said, nodding at Monica. "Everyone knows the Rozans are never hard up for money."

"Listen—"

"What do you want here?"

"Nothing. I just thought—"

"Whatever you're searching for isn't here." He turned away. "So go somewhere else."

"I just wanted to help out a friend."

William spun around and glared at him. "You don't have any friends here. You've never been one of us, and you don't belong." William's voice rose, gaining the attention of the clerk at the cash register and the two other customers. "Stop sweet-talking my wife and stay out of my business. I don't care if you throw around your money, but keep your advice to yourself." He stormed away.

JD watched him go with mixed emotions. He and William had never been close buddies, but they'd always been friendly to each other. Why the sudden change? What had made him so angry? Sure, he hadn't kept in touch as they'd agreed to as kids, but he'd never had much to say. He sighed. That was it. He'd lost touch. Their broken relationship was his fault, and he didn't blame William for feeling betrayed.

He'd done it wrong. He couldn't just walk into another man's life and tell him what to do. It was like holding up a mirror to his failures. He realized that his harsh approach could work in the city, but not here. And when it came to a man's pride, one had to tread carefully. He should have listened to Treena.

JD suddenly felt Monica's gentle touch on his shoulder. "You're supposed to be relaxing."

JD shrugged, trying to show a nonchalance he didn't feel. "He's right. I don't have friends. Especially not here. My father—" He abruptly stopped then picked up a squeaky dog toy and put it in the basket. "Let's go."

The young woman at the register had big green eyes and purple nail polish, and as she rang up the items she cast curious glances at Monica.

Monica adjusted her glasses. "What is it?"

"I'm just not used to seeing you with anybody. You always come in alone." She glanced at JD. "Are you two related or something?"

"No."

JD placed a candy bar on the counter. "We just happen to be living together."

Monica felt her face grow hot. "That's not…it's not… he's putting it in the wrong context."

The young girl stared at her blankly.

"He's staying for the summer."

She nodded with understanding. "Oh, right." She smiled at JD in recognition. "You're Ms. Nadine's grandson."

He returned her smile. "That's me."

"I figured it was something like that," she said, as if she'd finally uncovered the mystery of why the strange pair would be together.

Monica pursed her lips while JD tried hard to stifle back a laugh.

The clerk rang up everything and JD paid. "Thanks, Donna," he said, reading her name tag.

She beamed. "Come in anytime." She looked around then leaned forward. "And whatever advice you've got for this place, you can tell me. I really need this job, and Mr. Hostie isn't so bad when you get to know him."

"I'll remember that," JD said then followed Monica out of the store.

"Jealous?" JD teased as they headed toward the car.

"Of who?"

JD was about to reply when Drent Marks came from around the corner and spotted them. "You stupid bitch! You killed my dog," he said then threw his can of beer at her.

Chapter 4

Monica ducked before the beer can struck her in the face. The near miss only enraged Drent Marks further.

He was a big man, weighing nearly two hundred and eighty pounds, with a large knife tattoo on his neck and one of a daisy on his forearm. He punched his fist into the palm of his other hand. "Do you know how much you've cost me?"

JD stepped in front of Monica. "Drent, have you forgotten your medication?"

"Are you trying to be funny?"

"No, I'm trying to give myself a good reason not to beat the crap out of you for assaulting a woman."

"Get out of my way!"

JD folded his arms. "What's your problem?"

Drent pointed at Monica with fury. "That ugly little bitch just cost me a fortune!"

"Actually, she saved you from a lawsuit."

He paused. "A lawsuit? From who?"

"From me."

Monica stepped from around JD. "I'm not sorry I did it. Not only is it barbaric to use a puppy as bait to train your monsters, but to keep it tied up so that it can't run is worse than criminal, and I won't let that happen on my property."

"It isn't your property."

"I'm managing it for Ms. Rozan, and she wasn't pleased to learn that you'd been using her abandoned shed as a place for your dogfights, which are illegal in the state of Georgia."

Drent sniffed. "My cousin's the sheriff."

"That's an elected position, right?" JD said in a soft voice. "If he wants to serve for another term, he'll learn who he needs to please."

"Rozan, you may be powerful in the big city, but you'd better watch yourself out here."

"Do I look scared to you?"

Drent mimicked JD's stance and also folded his arms. "Just give me my property back and we're even."

"Your property?"

"Yeah." He gestured toward Baxter. "That's mine, too."

A sharklike grin spread on JD's face. "Want to fight me for him?"

Drent cracked his knuckles. "You wouldn't last a second."

"I'll last longer than you."

Drent flashed an ugly smile. "William told me about you. He said—"

"You can flatter me later. Let's go." JD handed Baxter over to Monica.

She looked at him, bewildered. She vigorously shook her head. "Oh, no. This is not a good idea. JD, I don't think—"

"I'll meet you around the corner in a minute," JD said to Drent and pointed to an alley near the store.

Drent laughed. "Make it two. I doubt you'll show up," he said then left.

JD headed for the car. "Open the trunk for me."

Monica hurried after him and said in a tense voice, "You don't need to do this." She lifted the trunk lid. "He's not worth it."

JD dumped the dog food inside then winced.

Monica noticed the reaction and swore. "You're not even fit to fight, and he's not going to fight fair."

JD slammed the lid closed. "Who says I'm going to be fair?"

He started to walk away then spun around and drew her to him. In one swift motion he covered her mouth with his in a quick, mind-numbing kiss. Just as quickly, he pulled away. "For good luck," he said then disappeared into the alley.

Monica didn't move at first, trying to gather her warring emotions—longing, annoyance, surprise, desire—then she swore and placed Baxter and some of the other items in the car. She left the window open a third of the way so that he could get air then locked the car, but not before taking out two large dog bones from one of the grocery bags. She gave one to the still-listless puppy and took the other with her as a make-shift weapon—then ran to the alley. The oily smell of diesel fuel reached her first, as well as the stench of days-old trash from overturned trash cans. Several pieces of sharp glass glinted from the sliver of sunlight that managed to seep between the buildings.

Monica focused her eyes and saw JD fighting Drent and two other guys. One of them looked like a teenager taken from a local wrestling team. The other man was smaller but thicker. Just as she'd feared, Drent wasn't fighting fair. But before she could run to help him, JD drop-kicked the smaller guy, head butted the other then grabbed Drent's fleshy neck and squeezed until he collapsed to the ground. JD bent over Drent and checked the fallen man's pulse. He nodded then stumbled back against the wall, and a pirate's grin spread across his face.

Monica's gaze swept over the three prone figures then settled on JD, unsure of whether she should be relieved or frightened. She'd known and seen another man who could be just as violent and brutal. The thought of him made her take a step back, and she dropped the bone. She quickly picked it up, but the sound caught JD's attention. He turned to her and frowned. "You were supposed to stay by the car."

"I thought you might need my help," she stammered, not wanting to have his temper directed at her.

JD pushed himself from the wall and walked up to her, as if sensing her unease. "You don't have to worry. He won't bother you again."

She glanced behind him. "We can't just leave them like this."

JD gently took her elbow and led her away. "Sure we can. Where's Baxter?"

"In the car. I made sure he's got enough air."

"Good. Let's go home."

Monica nodded, not trusting herself to speak. She let her gaze fall and noticed a red stain soaking through his shirt sleeve.

"You're bleeding again."

JD glanced down and swore. "At this rate I'm going to run out of shirts."

Monica reached over to examine the cut, but he stopped her. "Don't worry about it. I just want to get out of here." JD softened his tone with a wink. "You can nurse me at home."

Monica got in the driver's seat. "You could bleed to death before then."

"But you'd never let that happen," he said, fumbling with his seat belt.

Monica took the belt from him and locked it in place.

"See?" JD said. "I'm in good hands."

She started the ignition. After driving a few blocks, she said in a grim tone, "You enjoyed that, didn't you? You enjoy fighting."

JD shook his head. "No, I enjoy winning."

Monica fell quiet and tapped the steering wheel. "I think you should go."

He swung around to face her. "You too? Have you been talking to Hostie?"

"No, but he has the right idea. You should go somewhere else."

"Why?"

Monica threw up her hand in exasperation. "Just look at all the trouble you've caused in one day. You've gotten yourself stabbed, adopted a dog that's neurotic—"

"I'm only fostering him."

Monica continued. "Angered the guy at the one general store in town and antagonized a man whose cousin just happens to be the sheriff and then beat him and his friends unconscious."

"I tried to come up with a reason not to. You heard me."

"JD, I want a quiet life, and I know that will be impossible with you around. So I suggest you book a hotel on a nice island somewhere and relax there."

JD rested his head back. "It won't work."

"What?"

He grinned. "You can't get rid of me that easily."

"It's nothing personal."

JD lowered his voice, reached over and twirled a strand of loose hair around his finger. "Somehow I have a feeling that it is."

Monica slapped his hand away and tucked the wayward strand back under her head wrap. "What did I tell you about touching me?"

He rested back and stared out the window. "The truth is I don't want to be anywhere else but here."

"I thought you said there was nothing here."

He sent her a significant look. "I was wrong."

Monica focused on the road. No, she wouldn't fall for that. He was just trying to distract her from the truth. He had his secrets and so did she. Since he wasn't going to leave, she'd have to come up with another plan.

He had to get away before anyone could reach him. JD zipped up his carrying case—he didn't have time to pack anything bigger—then headed for the door. His cell phone rang. He saw the number and answered.

"Where are you?" his associate Cliff Englewood asked in a panic. "The Snyder meeting starts in ten minutes."

"Fill in for me. I'm taking a break."

"You can't do that now! You just put one of the most powerful men in jail and saved another company from ruin. People want to talk to you. You're news."

"I don't care." He was used to being news.

"Do you know how much this could cost you?"

"Not enough to make me come back right now." He wanted to get away from the journalists, associates and colleagues who all wanted something from him. People circled him like vultures would a dying man in a desert—if he didn't leave, he wouldn't have the energy to fight them all.

Someone knocked on the door. "Gotta go."

"JD, wait—"

"You can handle this. I trained you for this moment."

"I know but—"

"I've really gotta go." JD looked through the peephole and swore. Stacy. He'd forgotten to tell the front-desk security he wasn't seeing her anymore.

"What's wrong?"

"Trouble's just arrived. Take care of things. You'll be fine." He hung up then tapped his mobile phone against his chin, considering his options. He didn't have to answer, but she knew he was home and he'd have to face her eventually. He swore again, this time fiercely, hating the fact that he was trapped. He hid his travel bag in the closet and opened the door.

"I didn't expect to see you," he said. And hoped I never would again, he silently added as he opened the door wider for her to enter. She sauntered past, her spiked high heels clicking against his tiled floor and her devastating figure encased in a tight black dress. The sight left him cold.

"I have only one thing to say to you, you heartless bastard!" She lifted up a knife she'd kept hidden and lunged at him.

JD shot up from his bed—the pounding of his heart echoing in his ears, his breathing uneven. It was a dream. No. A nightmare, and it had been real. He rubbed his eyes then tried to adjust to his surroundings while a pale morning sun spilled onto the floor. He quickly assessed that he wasn't in his New York apartment with wraparound windows and its view of the city, but rather his grandmother's cozy farmhouse with its rustic furniture. He liked his room, except for the picture with an image of a musician; he wished his grandmother had left that one out. He glanced at his watch—5:30 a.m. He'd gone to bed at twelve, but he knew he wouldn't be able to go back to sleep. He fell back against the headboard and wiped the gleam of sweat from his forehead as his nightmare dissipated. Things had ended badly, but he had no regrets.

Stacy had called him heartless, but he doubted she even knew what a heart was used for. His tactic had been a bit ruthless, but he hadn't gotten as far as he had in life by being a nice guy. She was like all the rest: after him only for his money and position. But Stacy had wanted more—to have him save her father's company, which was admirable if her father hadn't been a criminal. She thought that being in his bed would blind him to what her father was up to, or tie him to her in some special way. She'd been wrong. She wasn't the first women in his life with a hidden agenda. Women always wanted something from him. Except Monica. At least for now.

No, Monica was different. She didn't care about his money or what he could do for her. She didn't even want him around. The thought made him smile. What kind of man would interest her? he wondered absently, stroking the wound she had rebandaged for him.

JD got out of bed, glanced at Baxter over in the corner fast asleep in his doggie bed. The first week with the puppy had been hard… He and Monica decided that they should set up Baxter's doggie bed in the kitchen, so that he could be around them most of the day. That was a disaster. Not only did he not like sleeping in the bed, every sound or noise sent him hurling himself under the large sofa in the family room, where he would remain for hours, forgoing water and food. They then decided to put his bed in the family room, but for some odd reason, he always ended up somehow getting into JD's bedroom and sleeping under his bed, so JD decided to let him stay. He didn't mind the company.

JD opened the window and inhaled the fresh country air and let the breeze sweep over him. He could breathe again. Yes, he'd made the right choice to leave the city without notice. He pictured his executive assistant, Pattie Brantford, scrambling to reschedule his appointments and calm the nerves of clients and associates, but she was good at that and he knew he'd left everything in capable hands. He needed to get away from it all and regroup. Maybe he could start feeling human again. He'd been living rote for the past few years and it was wearing on him. Especially after Stacy. He should have been wary of how aggressively she'd sought him out. He'd thought it was part of her charm at the time. As someone who went after what he wanted, he admired that trait in others. That had been a big error in judgment.

He watched the sun cascade over the lush grass and paint the top of trees a pale gold. He turned to Baxter, who looked at him with a curious expression. "Let's go for a walk."

Minutes later, he walked through the early morning dew-soaked grass. Baxter was a little hesitant at first, not liking to get his paws wet, but JD gave him no choice. He wouldn't wander toward the woods and would be more prepared this time. JD looked at the old chicken coop that now stood empty, remembering when he'd helped collect eggs as a boy. And the last walk he'd had with his dying father.

"I'm leaving you the man of the house now," his father said. "Look after your mother and your brother."

He fought back tears and nodded solemnly. "Yes, sir."

His father rested a heavy hand on his shoulder. "I've lived a good life. I wish I could stick around longer, but I guess God has other things for me to do." He smiled, and JD knew his father wanted him to smile too, but he refused. His father was everything to him and he hated the thought of losing him.

"I'll be looking down on you, you know that?"

"Yes, sir."

"I want you to promise me three things. You hear me?"

He nodded.

"You make sure your brother stays on the right path. Don't let him break your mother's heart. He's a wild one and will get into trouble if he's not watched carefully. You understand?"

JD nodded again. He knew what his father meant. His younger brother, Donnie, was a little too much like their uncle Billy, who'd spent three years in jail for fraud.

"Second, I want you to use that brain of yours to help people. There are enough selfish bastards in the world. I want you to leave a legacy of integrity. You have my name and I want you to use it well." His father turned away and stared up at the sky and sighed, his energy waning. His shirt hung on his thin frame, and although the weather was nearing eighty degrees, his father wore a long-sleeve shirt and worn wool sweater because he was always cold now. JD moved closer in case his father needed to lean on him.

His father cocked his ear. "Hear that? That's the sound of the gray catbird. It was named for its catlike call, but it can also mimic the sound of other birds and even some mechanical sounds. It likes to hide when it sings, too. Always reminds me that things aren't always as they seem." He looked at JD. "Whenever you hear it, think of me. And remember that things aren't always what they seem."

JD shifted from one foot to the other, feeling suddenly restless. "What's the third thing you want me to promise?"

His father knelt in front of him and gripped his shoulders. "Promise me you'll fight for happiness over anything else." He cupped his son's chin. "I worry about you. You're too focused, solemn and…" He sighed with frustration. "There are so many things I could show you about what life is. How you should live. I want you to smile at least twice a day, laugh at least five, whistle, listen to music." He tightened his hold, his voice urgent. "Live. For. Me."

It was too much. JD looked into his father's face and kind eyes and saw how pale the cancer had made him and how his skin stretched over his bones. He thought about staring at an empty place at the dinner table, a vacant seat in the church pew, of never walking with his father again. It was a promise he couldn't make. He'd never laugh or smile again. He shook his head and stepped away. "No."

His father reached for him. "JD—"

"No!" He yanked himself free. "I won't laugh. I won't smile. I won't whistle and you can't make me 'cause it's not fair. It's not fair!" He turned and ran. He knew his father couldn't catch him. He didn't want him to. He ran into the nearby woods and stomped on broken branches and kicked a nearby tree then fell to his knees and wept. "I'll never be happy again," he whispered, feeling his heart harden. He never wanted to love if it meant losing that person and feeling the terrible pain he felt now.

His father found him nearly twenty minutes later.

His face was lined with worry and his voice tinged with fear. "Don't ever run away from me again."

JD kept his gaze on the ground. "Yes, sir."

His father gathered him into his arms and JD felt tears filling his eyes, but this time he didn't pull away. He hugged him back, wishing he could keep his father alive forever.

"Be strong for me, son," his father said, his voice cracking with anguish. "Be strong for all of us."

"I will," JD said, knowing that was a promise he could keep. He would always be strong.

They left the woods and neither spoke about that conversation again. His father died a month later and as promised, JD looked after his brother, who continued to get into scrapes (nearly got shot for sleeping with a married woman, and was on his fourth job in two years) but nothing too serious.

His brother was now working as a building manager at one of JD's properties, and their mother was happy. As promised, he had also used his brain to help others by helping companies grow and, when needed, protecting them from corporate takeovers. He was established and successful and had never sullied his father's name.

But he knew he wasn't the man his father was. His father was life embodied. He could sparkle and laugh. JD couldn't remember the last time he'd been that carefree, but that didn't bother him. He'd never been lighthearted. It wasn't his nature and it wasn't what had gotten him this far.

However, he did like to make other people happy. Tonight he'd take his grandmother out and treat her to a movie. He couldn't remember the last time he'd gone out to eat that wasn't a business meeting. Even when he dined out with Stacy, those meetings always turned to business—her father's business. But with his grandmother, he knew it would be different. Being with her always lifted his spirits. She was a vibrant woman who, like his father, could find joy in simple things: a sunrise, a spring breeze. She'd urged her husband to buy the farmhouse as a refuge from her job as a professor of mathematics.

"Whenever you hear the gray catbird, think of me." He remembered his father's words and the sound of his voice. They seemed to echo in the silence, and for a moment he was a child again looking up at his father's face. But just as quickly, the image changed and he found himself staring up at a canopy of leaves. He didn't listen for the sound of the catbird because he didn't want to think about his father. Instead, he turned and walked back home.

Chapter 5

He was a man of his word; she had to give him that. Monica watched JD's car leave. He was on his way to take his grandmother to dinner and a movie. He'd offered to take her along, but Monica had politely refused. She'd stayed out of his presence as much as she could. After their first day together he'd busied himself with training Baxter, talking to his grandmother and roaming the property. Although she cooked dinner for two, they didn't eat together. She ate in her studio and he ate in the breakfast nook.

It would work, Monica thought with a satisfied sigh as she turned from the window. He hadn't asked to see her studio again, and she hoped he'd forgotten about it. A light tapping on the window caught her attention, and she saw that a light drizzle had started to fall. She opened the window and inhaled the scent of crisp, damp air and wet grass. She loved rainfall. She'd been born during the first rain after a two-month drought. Her parents believed she'd brought them luck, and she did.

From a little child, her beauty garnered attention. Her mother gave credit to her Native American heritage for her height and good skin. Her father claimed her African-American ancestors had given her her high cheekbones and almond-shaped eyes. But neither tried to take credit for her most unique feature—extraordinary hazel eyes that could at any given time be either emerald or gold. The women on both sides of her family had thick long hair, but hers cascaded down her back like an onyx river.

It was her grandmother who first saw her potential to make money and urged her mother to put her in modeling. Money was tight so her mother readily agreed. Monica didn't even need to audition. Her mother took a snapshot and sent it to a few agents. Within days they had offers and within a week she was working. At six her childhood freedom came to an abrupt halt. Soon she was supporting the family with her work in print ads and commercials. She'd never been allowed to do what other kids did. She was kept indoors like a china doll. She was allowed to swim to keep toned but she could not climb trees, ride a bicycle or go skating. Nothing that could lead to scraped knees or elbows. Her skin had to be perfect.

Her mother and grandmother hovered over her like two protective hens, and she knew her importance to them and the family budget. She was the light while her younger sister, Nikki, was almost a shadow. Her sister didn't seem to mind, because she was free to be

a regular child. She could go to the park and the play-
ground. She even went to the local school while Monica
was given lessons at home. Nikki would leave the house
and come back with tales of her adventures at the jungle
gym or school, and Monica eagerly listened to a life
that couldn't be hers.

It had been over a year since she'd last seen her
sister, at Delong's funeral. Nikki had been cordial to
Delong. She found him fascinating but never really
liked him. He'd discovered Monica at fifteen. He was
a wealthy artist who first mentored her then became
her lover and finally her husband. He exposed her to
a world beyond her Oklahoma and New Jersey childhood. He made her more than a model. Through his
guidance and brilliance he made her an icon. She was
featured in music videos, movies and art exhibitions.
She developed a clothing line and had enterprises in
perfume and cosmetics. Together they owned several
cars and five homes.

"But none of them are you," Nikki once said when
she came to visit Monica's New Jersey residence.

"But I love them. Especially this one," Monica said,
wanting to convince her sister of her happiness.

"It's not a true home," she said, casting a glance at
the stained glass and arched windows. "Your spirit and
personality aren't anywhere in this house. You're just
part of the collection."

"I'm his wife, not his possession."

"You think he knows the difference?"

"You just don't understand him." She knew Nikki
couldn't. Few people could. Delong was larger than
life—a bold and passionate man. Their marriage wasn't

normal, because Delong wasn't a normal man. She knew there were other women but it wasn't often, and she was his wife and that's what mattered. When he strayed, he always came back to her with gusto. Besides, she needed him kept occupied because she had her own career and busy schedule, which at times could be exhausting. She knew there would never be any children. Taking care of Delong and his sometimes volatile moods was enough for her. Her sister was wrong. Delong loved her. He was a genius whose life was just as much his art as his work. She didn't care what color he painted the walls or what furniture he bought. He took good care of her and life was perfect.

"Just let me decorate one room for you," Nikki said.

"All right," Monica replied, knowing that her sister, a top interior designer, wanted to do something special for her. Delong was in Venezuela, so Nikki could make changes without interference.

Monica allowed her sister to redecorate a small room near the back of the house in sweeping colors. Monica loved it. Delong didn't. He never said so, but his silence was eloquent enough. Within a week of his return, Delong found a better use for the room. He used it to store his sculptures. And he didn't stop until every hint of Nikki's original design was gone.

"That bastard," Nikki said when she saw the room later that year. "Your one little corner in this mausoleum and he took it."

"It wasn't deliberate," Monica said with a tired sigh, not understanding her sister's anger. It was just a room. She had plenty of others.

"Yes, it was. He has to be the center of everything."

"I don't know why you don't like him."

Nikki turned away. "And I don't know why you do."

Her sister had left angry that day, and at the funeral their meeting had been strained. Nikki tried but couldn't hide her relief that he was gone, and that hurt Monica. She'd wanted someone to share his memory with, but her parents were dead. They'd had the two of them later in life and had passed away in their late seventies. They'd lived long enough to see Monica married and her career take off. They were proud and happy for her. Nikki wasn't, and that sore spot hadn't healed.

Monica looked around her bedroom with its simple decor. Delong would think that it was ugly and plain, and he'd think the same of the disguise she now wore. But it felt right. For a moment she wondered what Nikki would do to the room and what creative magic she would work in this small space. She missed her. It had taken time, but she now understood why her sister had so fiercely wanted her to have her own room. But she'd been so used to being an extension of someone else it had never crossed her mind to have something of her own. Now she wanted that and couldn't.

The farmhouse wasn't her home. Would any place ever be truly hers? She closed the window, as if doing so also shut out her past, and for the next hour and a half Monica worked in her studio. She stopped when she heard a car drive up.

She looked out her window and saw JD get out of the car. Her curiosity grew. What was he doing home already? She glanced at her watch and frowned. There was no way he could have done dinner and a movie in that short amount of time. What had happened? She turned from the window and shook her head. It was none of her business. What he did in his spare time didn't matter to her. But although she tried to focus on her work, her curiosity about his unexpected return wouldn't disappear. Resigned, Monica went downstairs just in time to see JD refilling Baxter's water bowl.

"Wasn't the movie any good?" she asked him.

JD looked up, surprised to see her. She didn't blame him. Except for cursory remarks like "hi" or "good morning," she hadn't engaged him in conversation.

"Gran wasn't feeling well so I just ordered something in then played for her."

"Played for her? What did you play?"

He folded his arms and a slow smile touched his lips. "I'll tell you if you'll show me your studio."

Damn, he hadn't forgotten. "I'm not *that* interested."

JD shrugged then went into the family room. Monica swore because she knew that he'd gotten her. Her imagination would race until she discovered what he'd played for his grandmother. She reluctantly followed him into the other room and saw him reading a book on dog training. Although he looked casual, something about him was different. More subdued. She again wondered why he was here. What was he running away from? She knew he had his reasons why he wanted to hide, but it wasn't just overwork; she understood because she had her own dark reasons. "Okay, you win," she said.

"Good." He tossed the book aside and stood up as if she'd said exactly what he'd expected. For a moment Monica wondered if his subdued look had been a trap.

"Tell me what you played first."

JD shook his head. "After I see the studio. I wouldn't want you to change your mind."

Monica rested her hands on her hips, affronted. "I wouldn't—"

He held up his hand, firm. "That's the deal."

Monica sighed fiercely then marched up the stairs. If he wanted to see her studio, fine. He wouldn't uncover anything exciting there. Just equipment and jewelry designs. She had nothing to worry about. He wouldn't stay long. He'd just have a quick look around and then he'd be gone. But that thought didn't stop her from being aware of how close he was to her as he followed and how he seemed to loom over her. It was an amazing feat, because he was only a couple of inches taller than she was, but he commanded the space around him. She took a deep breath then opened the door.

JD walked in and looked around. Monica quickly scanned the space to make sure everything was in its place. She liked to keep things meticulous. A large magnifying glass stood attached to her drawing table, and several old clothes and a worn apron hung on pegs off to the side. Sheets of silver sat sorted by size and were filed neatly in a freestanding organizer. Several pliers, a small hammer and a torch for soldering lay neatly on a workbench situated in the middle of the room directly under a skylight. Several bottles, clearly labeled, were lined up on the table next to small remnants of jewelry she had been working on, and at the back of the studio was a double sink.

Monica couldn't read anything from JD's expression. She folded her arms, regretting letting him in. Was he going to judge her or be politely condescending?

"I'm the artist, darling, and you're merely my creation," Delong liked to say in an indulgent tone when she offered him a design or tried to sketch something of her own. *"Why do you need to create art when you're a masterpiece?"*

"These are just sketches of new designs," she said when JD lingered over her drawing table. His silent study grated on her nerves.

"And this is a custom-made design for a client. I sell my items on consignment through a small gift shop in town, and I have an associate who takes several of my pieces to local art shows and sells them there."

JD watched her with such intensity she suddenly felt tongue-tied. "It's a good business," she said defensively.

"I didn't say it wasn't," he said in a low voice.

"You haven't said anything."

"Because I don't know what to say. You sell locally?"

"Yes," she said, proud that her work was selling.

"Why not expand?"

"Because I don't want to."

"You should." He shrugged. "I'd expected some cute homemade trinkets, but these are stunning. Museum quality. You shouldn't only be selling them to tourists and secondhand shoppers. These are world class. It's evident that you've studied internationally. I haven't seen patterns like this since my trip to Benin and Nigeria." He lifted a sketch and moved over to the light. "This one makes me think of Marrakech—the fusion of artistic vision captured in one small object. What's your company called?"

"The Silver Stone."

He nodded. "Good. It rings true." He sat down at her drawing table. "What was the inspiration behind this?" He gestured to a set of earrings.

"The peacock. I was traveling in Malaysia and I saw one and it captivated me. The colors were extraordinary."

"Yes, I can see that. Put them on for me."

Monica stared at him for a moment, not sure she'd heard him correctly. "Why?"

"Because I'm thinking of buying them as a gift for a friend and want to see if the set will work."

An intimate friend? Monica wanted to ask then scolded herself for even caring. Of course he did. He probably had several. He was an attractive man. Even she had nearly fallen under the spell of his casual flirtation. And she wouldn't think about the kiss. He'd never mentioned it because it had been an impulsive act that hadn't meant anything. But there was no way she'd put on her creations and be compared to the glamorous and stylish women he knew. "Use your imagination."

"I just want to see them on a real person."

"It will be like draping crystal around a tree trunk."

"You're a lot prettier than a tree trunk and this will take less than a minute. Your ears are pierced, so you must have worn jewelry at some point. Come on," he said in a silky, persuasive voice.

Monica sighed then put the earrings on. He helped her clasp the matching necklace, the knuckles of his hand brushing against her skin, causing it to tingle. She abruptly turned to him, steeling herself from his affect on her. "There," she said in a sharp tone, trying to be nonchalant. "Doesn't that give you an idea?"

JD rubbed his chin, letting his gaze roam over her in a slow, lazy appraisal, making her body grow warm as the seconds stretched. "No, that won't work." He looked at another pair. "Try this set."

She hesitated. "I don't—"

"Just one more," he said in the same silky voice.

Reluctantly, Monica obliged, and again his penetrating gaze seemed to undress her, peeling the layers back off her ugly paisley dress and tinted glasses as though he could see who she really was. He looked at her as if she was stunningly beautiful, and it frightened her.

He shook his head again and smiled. "Why don't we—"

It was the smile that did it. It was superior and smug, and she realized it had all been a game. JD hadn't been looking at her with any real interest. She'd let her vanity make her a fool. She wasn't Venus. Just Monica, and Monica was a laughable, pitiable creature who no man had glanced at in months. The sharp sting of humiliation pierced her then turned to anger. "Get out."

He blinked. "What?"

Monica shoved him toward the door. "I said get out!" She shoved him harder, as if trying to get rid of not only him, but also the feelings he had stirred up in her. "I thought you were different, but you're just like all the rest. Did you enjoy your little game? Was it fun to mock me? It was like dressing up a dog, wasn't it?"

JD widened his eyes, stunned. "That's not what—"

"You knew in an instant whether the necklace would work against your friend's long, smooth neck, how the earrings would dangle against her perfect jawline, but you had to try it out on me—the plain woman—so you could laugh at the stark contrast." She shoved him again.

JD stumbled back into the hallway. "Monica—"

"'How could someone so ordinary, so sheltered, create such beautiful things?' you thought. I know your type—arrogant and condescending. The world revolves around you, and everyone else should just get out of your way." She tapped her chest. "I'm proud of my business. It may be local and small, but it's mine and that means a lot. I don't care what you think of it or me or about your big companies and fine women. You're no better than—" She stopped before she said Anton's name and steadied her voice. "I'm sorry I ever trusted you. It was a foolish mistake I won't make again." She slammed the door shut. JD swung it back open with such force she stumbled back and fell to the ground. He approached her and she held her hands up, ready to defend herself.

JD squatted in front of her, his gaze soft and his voice tender. "What the hell did he do to you to make you so afraid?"

Monica slowly let her hands fall. "I don't know what you're talking about."

"Yes, you do. What's his name?"

"It doesn't matter," she said, in no mood to argue with him. "It was a long time ago."

"But you're still afraid."

"I'm not afraid. Just cautious."

JD seized her arm and she screamed out in alarm. He immediately released her. "You call that cautious?"

"You surprised me, that's all," she said, embarrassed by her reaction. *He must think I'm crazy.*

"I've never hit a woman in my life." He nodded to his wound. "And trust me, I've had reason to."

"It's not that."

He held out his hand. "Why don't we start again as friends?"

Monica lowered her gaze.

JD dropped his hand. "For the last several days you've treated me like a pariah and I've left you alone, but we'll be sharing this space for about two months. I'm not going to pretend that you don't exist, and I want you to do the same."

Monica scrambled to her feet and dusted off her dress, wishing he didn't sound so sincere.

JD didn't stand. He remained kneeling and looked up at her, bewildered. "I like you, okay? Really. It surprised the hell out of me, too. You're not my type at all, but there's something about you." He shook his head, amazed. "I can't explain it." He rose to his feet. "I like you. It's as simple as that, and if you gave me a chance I think you'd like me, too."

Monica folded her arms and turned away. She did like him. That was the problem. She liked him more than she wanted to. This wasn't supposed to happen.

She squeezed her eyes shut. "I'm just not used to this."

JD walked up behind her, close but not touching. "I could make you get used to it real fast." He slowly turned her around to face him. "I think you're wonderful," he said then his lips covered hers like hot caramel over ice cream, his bottom lip as soft as she'd remembered and as delicious as ripened strawberries. He sent her senses spinning.

Wonderful? He thought she was wonderful? No man had ever said that to Monica. To Venus? Yes. Always to Venus. As Venus she'd been called spectacular, exquisite, dazzling, gorgeous. Men had complimented her on everything from her eyes to her ankles. Adoration was a given, but after months living in this small town as Monica Dulane, not one man had complimented her or given her a second look, which was the way she wanted it to be.

JD had changed all that. Here was a man telling and showing her how wonderful he thought she was. Just the way she was. He wrapped his arms around her, pressing his solid form against her until she felt the evidence of his desire, and her own body grew warm and wet with wanting. Yes, she wanted him. She opened her mouth to receive him farther inside, and his moan of pleasure was all the encouragement she needed. Monica snaked an arm around his neck. "This is probably a mistake."

"I don't make mistakes, just calculated risks."

"I'm a big risk."

"I can take whatever you give me."

"We'll see about that." She jumped up and wrapped both legs around his waist then covered his mouth again. He cupped his hands under her bottom and then her thighs, matching her passion with his own. She kissed a sensitive part behind his ear. He nearly lost his balance and fell against the wall. The impact made her head wrap come loose, but she didn't care. She could ride him for miles.

Monica ripped open his shirt and took one of his nipples into her mouth and let her tongue tease it. And she would have done a lot more, if her glasses hadn't started sliding off her face. She quickly remembered where she was and *who* she was supposed to be: Monica. Shy, retiring Monica would not suck a man's nipples and ride him like a bronco.

Monica abruptly pulled away and shoved her glasses back on her face, appalled by her behavior. "I'm so sorry."

JD stared at her, startled and breathless. "About what? That was amazing." His eyes scanned the length of her as though removing her clothing. "You're amazing." He pushed himself from the wall and walked toward her with purpose.

Monica took a hasty step back. "My God, what do you see?"

JD halted and furrowed his brows. "What?"

Monica threw out her arms, wanting to laugh. It was so absurd that this gorgeous man was attracted to her. She saw the night sky behind him and thought of A *Midsummer Night's Dream.* Clearly a trickster was creating havoc in her life, just as he had in that play where the fairy queen fell in love with the ugly character Bottom. It was as if JD was under a spell. "Tell me what you see that's so wonderful." She let her hands fall. "I'm plain. I'm fine with that. I'm twenty pounds overweight—"

JD shook his head. "You're not overweight. You're just the right size."

She ignored him. "I wear dull clothes, tinted glasses—"

"Why do you have to wear them?"

Monica paused, surprised by the question. Hadn't Nadine told him? "I'm sensitive to light."

"Even in the house? I could make the lights dim."

She adjusted her head wrap. "I'm sensitive to all kinds of light."

"Oh."

Monica scratched her head. "Now what was I saying?"

"I don't remember."

She narrowed her eyes, catching his quick grin. "I do. I was talking about what you see in me. How we're completely mismatched because I'm plain and—"

"So what?"

"What?"

"You don't seem to care, so why should I?" He pressed a finger to her lips before she could argue. "Let me tell you what I see. I see a confident woman who can handle a rifle when she needs to. A smart woman who runs her own business. A talented woman who creates extraordinary jewelry, and a woman with lips that taste so sweet she leaves me hungry for more."

His mouth covered hers again. She didn't stop him. If he was under a spell, so was she. Delong had been her only lover and he'd been ardent and sensual, but he'd never made her feel like this.

JD's lips slid to her neck. "I could strip you naked right now."

"But you won't."

"I will next time."

And she wanted him to. But not now. She had to plan it. She had to be careful. Monica drew away. "We'd better stop."

"Why?"

"Because you're scaring me."

He stepped back, startled and concerned. "What?"

Monica shook her head, regretting her choice of words. "No, not you…I mean this. It's all happening too fast."

JD let out a deep breath. "All right, we'll take it slow. Just give me a minute. Let the beast go back in its cage."

"You call it a beast?"

"Only when it's disappointed."

She caressed his cheek. "I'm sorry."

"You're not helping matters by touching me like that."

She snatched her hand away. "I'm—"

"And don't apologize again. I understand—I don't like it—but I do." He traced the pattern of her necklace with his finger. "It's beautiful, but if I were to buy you jewelry, it would be a simple set of pearls—elegant, simple and exquisite."

"You have a tongue made of honey."

He winked. "You should know."

Monica felt her face grow hot thinking of what his tongue had been up to, but she didn't turn away. She took his hand. "I'm hungry. Let's eat."

JD wasn't hungry so Monica made a simple meal of a grilled cheese sandwich and bowl of tomato soup for herself. They went into the family room and watched a *NOVA* special. Although the program was interesting, JD seemed especially quiet. He stared at the screen but his attention seemed to be elsewhere. Was he brooding because she'd halted what they'd been doing upstairs?

She remembered that her husband could sulk for days if he didn't get his way.

"Do you want to change the station?" she asked.

"No, it's fine."

She sighed. "I know you're annoyed with me for stopping everything, but it really was moving too fast."

He turned to her. "I'm not annoyed."

Monica began to relax. "Then why have you been so quiet? What's wrong?"

"I was thinking about Gran." He hesitated. "I'm worried about her. She didn't seem herself tonight, and I hated leaving her alone."

"Invite her over for dinner tomorrow."

He raised his eyebrows. "You wouldn't mind?"

"Of course I wouldn't mind. Why would I?"

"I know how much you like your privacy and space."

"I've grown to love her. If it hadn't been for her, I wouldn't have a place to stay."

JD leaned over and kissed Monica on the cheek then stood and pulled out his cell phone. "Thanks. I'll call her right now." He disappeared into the other room.

Monica touched her cheek like a moonstruck teenager who'd been kissed by a rock star. The feel of his lips made her want to tell him the truth.

"Monica?"

She turned and saw JD frowning, the phone pressed to his chest. "She won't come?" she asked him.

He shook his head and his frown deepened. "No," he replied. "It's not that. She's determined to be the one to cook dinner."

Monica held out her hand. "Give me the phone."

JD hesitated. "She's stubborn."

"And I'm no pushover." Monica took the phone from him. "Nadine, *I'm* cooking dinner."

"Do you like him?" Nadine asked.

Monica paused, shocked by the question. "What?"

"You heard me. JD. Do you like him?"

Monica glanced at him. "I can't answer that right now."

"He's still there?" Nadine said with delight.

"We're supposed to be talking about dinner."

"Oh," Nadine said with a dismissive tsking sound. "I only said I'd cook as an excuse to get you on the phone."

"Nadine," Monica said with warning.

The older woman giggled like a naughty girl. "He's everything I told you and more, right?"

Monica decided to change the topic. "I heard that you weren't feeling well."

"Just a little bug. Don't worry about me. It's you two I'm concerned about."

"Don't be. We're fine."

"So you *do* like him?"

Monica sighed and glanced at JD. He smiled as if he knew—and expected—he would be the subject of their conversation.

"Yes."

"How much?"

"Nadine!"

"All right, I'll find out later. I'm just glad you two are getting along. At first I was afraid, because—"

JD snatched the phone away from her. "Gran, are you talking about me?" He paused and wiggled his brows at Monica. "I can tell because you're making her blush."

Monica held out her hand. "Give me the phone."

He sat down. "We're getting on just fine," he said, pulling Monica down on his lap.

She tried to wiggle free but JD wrapped his arm tighter around her waist, trapping her. "No, we get on like two peas in a pod." He held the phone to his chest. "Gran wants to know if we want blackberry or pecan pie."

Monica glared at him.

He nodded as if she'd given him an answer and returned to the phone. "Make both. We'll decide when you get here." He stiffened and his voice suddenly changed. "What do you mean you're not coming?"

JD loosened his hold on Monica and she jumped off his lap, yanked the phone from him and said, "Nadine, you're coming tomorrow." JD reached for the phone, but Monica held out her hand and said in a low warning tone, "Remember, I know how to use a rifle."

"What?" Nadine said, alarmed.

"I wasn't talking to you," Monica said with a superior smile while JD returned to his seat.

"Good. I'll see you two in a couple of weeks."

"A couple of weeks? Why?"

"I just need some more time to get over this bug, and then it takes time for me not to still be contagious, so I should be all better by then. In the meantime you two can get to know each other a little more."

Monica sighed. Her friend's matchmaking effort was as subtle as a slingshot. "Nadine—"

"Talk to you later," she said then hung up.

Monica disconnected the phone then shook her head. "You're right," she said, handing him the phone. "Your grandmother is stubborn. She's not coming until Saturday—two weeks from now. She says she'll feel better then."

JD scratched his chin, concerned. "Maybe I should visit her tomorrow."

"I think she's trying to give us more time alone. Don't worry. If she was seriously ill she would tell us, but she sounded like her old self on the phone."

JD nodded. "You're right."

"What did you play for her?" Monica asked, wanting to remove the worried expression that lingered in his eyes.

JD stretched his arms the length of the couch. "The guitar."

Monica looked at him, surprised. He seemed like the type of man who'd spend years learning classical piano or the violin, not an earthy instrument like the guitar.

He caught her expression and grinned. "Yes, that's what I thought you'd think. I don't seem the type, I know. My father—" He stopped. "Anyway I don't play as much as I used to. I only did it because it makes Gran happy. She keeps one in the house."

"I'd love to hear you play."

JD opened his mouth and at first Monica was sure he'd say no. Then he slowly nodded his head as if coming to a decision. "Perhaps one day."

Perhaps wasn't yes, and Monica knew there were still parts of his life he was hesitant to share with her. They were still strangers, and that brief interlude upstairs hadn't changed that. She suddenly felt awkward, not knowing what to do next. Dinner was over and she had no reason to stay. She began to gather her dishes.

"No," JD said. "Leave them for later."

"But—"

JD patted the space beside him. "Just sit here with me."

Monica hesitated then sat, and JD rested his arm around her shoulders. It felt solid and warm and she began to relax and watch TV. She'd never done something this simple with a man before. She was used to performances. With Delong she was his audience. He was set on impressing her with flights in private jets, helicopter rides, fine dining on balconies that overlooked exotic locales, expensive boating trips, and she'd reward him with her smiles and listen to him as if he was the most important person in the world. But not JD.

He didn't seek out to dazzle her, and she didn't have to perform for him. No coy laughs or sexy flips of her hair. He liked her company, he'd said. He thought she was talented and smart and brave. He made her feel beautiful in a completely different way.

"Oh, I almost forgot," JD said then reached into his pocket. He pulled out some brightly colored stones— smoothly polished and beautiful—and placed them in her lap. "For inspiration."

Monica looked down and wanted to laugh. She'd once had a tycoon do the same gesture, except he'd offered her sapphires and diamonds. But what JD had given her meant much more.

She lifted a purplish stone. "They're beautiful. Where did you find these?"

"There's a creek two miles from here, and I saw

them and thought you might like them. My father and I used to—" He bit his lip. "I hope you'll find them useful."

"I will. Thank you."

JD flashed a brief smile then returned to watching TV.

Monica knew the next step was up to her. She could keep this relationship going or let it fade. He'd done his part with this offering. Now it was up to her. She took a deep breath then said, "Tomorrow could you show me where you found them?"

His eyes met hers, shining bright with mischief and desire, and for the second time that day she felt as if she'd fallen into a trap. But his tone gave nothing away when he softly said, "I'd love to."

Chapter 6

The next morning their walk was quiet, but Monica didn't mind. She didn't find JD's quiet mood unsettling. It allowed her to bask in the morning sun, listen to stray branches snap under their steps and watch Baxter scamper alongside them. They came upon a worn path where they had to duck several times to avoid being smacked in the face by low-hanging branches with broad, untamed leaves. They were surrounded by tall willows, old oak trees and numerous pine trees.

Suddenly JD stopped and pointed. "There."

Monica looked in the direction and saw a beautiful creek bed littered with colorful stones. She sat down on a rock while Baxter busied himself digging for something. She smiled at his efforts, took off her shoes and sunk her feet into the water. "Oh, it feels nice."

"My father used to—" JD stopped and shoved his hands in his pockets.

Monica sent him a curious look. "Why do you do that?"

"Do what?"

"Stop talking every time you mention your father."

"I do?"

She nodded.

JD shrugged with nonchalance. "Habit, I guess. I'm just not used to talking about him."

He didn't say any more than that and Monica shifted her position, wondering if she should push him to share. But as the silence grew, she felt she had no choice. "When did he die?"

"A long time ago."

The wall he'd erected around himself was firmly in place, but that didn't intimidate her. It made her more determined. "That doesn't matter. Time doesn't erase the pain."

JD sat on a boulder beside her. "You sound like someone who understands."

"I do. I've lost people I loved." Before he could ask who, Monica asked, "So how old were you?"

"Nine." He sighed then looked around him. "This was our special place. We used to enjoy skipping stones."

"What?"

"Skipping stones."

"How do you skip a stone?"

JD looked at her as if she'd suddenly spouted gibberish. "Are you serious?"

"Yes, I don't know what you're talking about."

He bent down and picked up a small, smooth stone then skimmed it over the water.

Monica's face lit up. "Oh, yes! I've seen that done on TV."

"On TV? You've never skipped stones before?"

"No, but it looks easy." She picked up a stone and threw it. It sank under the water. Another attempt garnered the same result. She frowned. "I don't understand."

JD laughed at her frustration. "There's a method to it. It's in the wrist."

Monica tried again and the stone sank once again.

"I'll show you." He came up behind her and took her hand in his. "It's the wrist action that counts and how you angle yourself."

His voice was neutral but his body was warm, making it hard for Monica to concentrate. His hands were big, but soft, and they slid down her arms then settled around her waist. He placed a kiss on the back of her neck.

She spun around. "That's not fair."

"Who said I wanted to play fair?"

Monica held out the stone. "You're supposed to teach me how to skip stones."

"I'll teach you another time."

"You already have." She turned and skipped a stone four times then sent him a smug grin.

JD stared openmouthed then looked at her. "You little fake."

She laughed. "I can fake a lot of things." She placed a finger under his chin and whispered. "Especially when it comes to stroking a man's ego."

JD seized her wrist and pulled her close. "You'd better not fake with me."

"You'd never know."

"With me you'll never have to."

She believed him and for a second pictured him naked, in her bed, his body covering hers while he went deep inside her. The thought made her temperature rise and she would have fanned herself if she'd been alone. But his piercing dark eyes studied her every movement, so she took a deep breath and smiled, as if she found his challenge amusing, then slipped out of his grasp. Monica sat back down on a rock and drew up her legs to create distance from him. "What else did you and your father do?"

JD paused as if trying to adjust to the abrupt change in conversation. "Hike. He used to teach me dirty limericks."

"Do you remember any?"

"No."

"You're lying."

JD's mouth spread into a grin, but he didn't reply.

"I'll get some out of you one day."

"Maybe." He sat down beside her, his back touching her arm. He wouldn't allow distance to separate them, and at that moment she felt no need to move away. She knew and accepted that she would sleep with him. Not tonight, but some night soon. It would be a risk, but she knew she wouldn't regret it. At her moment of awakening she heard the sound of the gray catbird and glanced up. "Oh, I've always loved that sound."

JD spun to her. "What did you say?"

Monica hesitated, startled by the intensity of his gaze, aware of how close his face was to hers. So close she could see silver specks in his brown eyes. She pointed to a tree. "I was just referring to the sound of the birdsong."

"It was my father's favorite, too." He stood and shoved his hands in his pockets. "I never thought I'd be able to come back here and feel happy again. But I do, and it's because of you."

"No, it's—"

He pulled her to her feet. "All my life I've been searching for something—something warm and wonderful and real, something I'd thought I'd lost when my father died, and I've finally found it again."

Monica shook her head, feeling uneasy. He was giving her credit she didn't deserve. She wasn't real. She was a fraud. "I think you're exaggerating."

"Don't argue with me," he said then didn't give her a chance to. For the next several minutes he kept her mouth occupied.

At last she drew away, breathless and weak in the knees. "JD, I—"

"I'm not seeing anyone, in case you were wondering."

"I wasn't actually, but—"

"Do you have a favorite restaurant where I could take you?"

"JD, be sensible."

"Do you like flowers? You look like the dandelions type."

"Dandelions are weeds."

"Daffodils then."

She sighed. "You're relentless."

He grinned. "Now you're starting to understand me." He took her hand. "Let's go home."

Monica looked down at their locked hands. "You don't have to do that."

JD blinked with a look of innocence. "I wouldn't want you to get lost."

Monica shook her head, amused. "You're a sly devil."

"And you're not afraid of me."

"No."

"But something about me frightens you. What is it?"

"Nothing."

He studied her for a long moment then whispered, "I'll figure it out."

Monica only smiled. *Not if I can help it.*

Going for walks soon became routine and a chance for JD to work with Baxter. However, one day nearly changed that. The three of them had gone for a walk, along the woods behind the farmhouse, and after strolling for about fifteen minutes JD realized Baxter was nowhere to be seen.

"Baxter… Come here, boy," he called out.

No reply.

"He must be busy trying to bury something," Monica said, because the puppy loved to take twigs and bury them, just as he would if they were bones.

"But we usually see him do it," JD said, looking around. He gave a loud whistle and yelled, "Baxter, come here, boy."

Monica grabbed JD's arm. "What if Drent got him? Maybe he was kidnapped."

"Kidnapped?" JD said with a sniff. "That's a bit dramatic, don't you think?"

Monica shrugged. "You don't know what people are capable of."

"He wouldn't be that stupid. And if he is, I'll knock some sense into him." He halted. "Hear that?"

She stopped too and listened.

They both heard the faint sound of something whining somewhere behind them. As they walked toward the sound, Monica looked down and saw a gray catbird inside a bush imitating the whining sound of a puppy.

"It's not him," Monica said, pointing toward the bush. The bird flew off.

JD frowned. "Clever little—"

Monica touched his sleeve. "Wait. I still hear something."

She searched around and then saw Baxter. Or rather the back of him. He was tightly wedged in a small fox hole, face-first. He had been pinned for some time, and they wouldn't have heard him had it not been for the bird. It took some ingenious digging to get him out, and afterward JD gave him a long bath.

"Little troublemaker," JD said as he dried him off.

"You're well matched," Monica teased. "Serves you right. You thought that being a foster parent would be easy."

"You don't think I can train him, do you?"

"I think you'll try very hard."

And he did, but he quickly discovered that Baxter didn't like squeaky toys. If any of them made the faintest sound, he was off running, terrified that the toy was real and after him.

"I guess this is what first-time parenthood feels like," JD said one day when they could not coax the puppy from behind a small space between a side table and side wall.

"It's going to take time," Monica said. "Living with Drent and his horrid gang must have been hell. Remember, you said you'd be patient."

"I was wrong." He finally got Baxter out of his hiding place and cradled him in his arms.

Monica saw the dog begin to relax. "He likes when you hold him. You're good for him."

JD shook his head. "He's even afraid of his own shadow." He picked up one of his dog-training manuals. "I must be doing something wrong. Maybe I need to hire a dog expert."

None of the experts JD hired—a dog trainer, a dog counselor and dog handler—thought they could help him. All three told him that based on Baxter's earlier experience as a bait dog, he was beyond help.

But JD refused to give up, and Monica admired his tenacity. When he finally hired a dog acupuncturist, they started to see progress, but not fast enough for JD. He decided to look at the situation from a different angle and finally hit on the perfect solution.

"What have you done to him?" Monica asked when she met JD on the porch to go for their walk. She looked down at Baxter, who wore a doggie coat with two large pockets on the side filled with twigs.

"I'm giving him a job. I thought of him as one of my employees."

"An employee?"

"Yes. If I had an employee I knew was capable but who was insecure, what would I do with him? I'd give him a job that made him feel good about himself."

He nodded down at the dog. "That's what I'm doing with him. He now has a job carrying the twigs into the forest. See? His tail is already up. He's proud of himself."

"You did it. I'm impressed."

"So impressed that you'll give me a kiss?"

Monica leaned forward and kissed him on the cheek.

He frowned. "I expected you to be more impressed than that."

She took his hand. "I will be after your grandmother's visit. Come on, Baxter is eager to go."

"You've cast my grandson under a spell," Nadine said as she and Monica stacked the dirty dishes in the dishwasher.

Monica kept her face averted. "I don't know what you mean."

"You know exactly what I mean." She started tugging at Monica's head wrap.

Monica straightened and stared down at the older woman. "What are you doing?"

Nadine frowned. "You really should try a less severe style, soften your looks."

"I kept it loose especially for you."

Nadine shrugged. "I suppose it doesn't matter. He likes you just the way you are." She nodded as though coming to a conclusion. "Yes, he must see past all this the way I do." She touched Monica's sleeve. "Thank you. I haven't seen him so relaxed and happy in a long time, and I worry…" She sighed, suddenly looking old. "I haven't seen him smile like this since… It's been too long. You're good for him. Thank you."

"I haven't done anything," Monica said, shocked by the older woman's praise. "It's his work with Baxter that's made him this way. He's done wonders with that little dog, and Baxter follows him everywhere. Plus, he's happy because you're here. He truly cares about you."

"I know," Nadine said with another heavy sigh. "But don't sell yourself short. You've done more for him than you know. It's a day I've lived for. He's going to need you."

Monica was about to ask her about her somber words, but JD entered the kitchen and said, "I thought you might need some help cutting the pies."

"You mean you want to get your big share," Monica said.

Nadine picked up a tea tray. "I'll take this into the other room." She scurried out.

JD watched Monica take the pie out of the oven. "Talking about me again?"

"Your ego is amazing. There are other topics of conversations between two women."

"So that would be a yes." He looked at the three pies. "She went overboard again."

"It makes her happy."

JD bit his lip. "Does she seem okay to you?"

"She seems a little tired, but she's still recovering from that bug that hit her."

"Hmm…she's thinner than I remember, but I haven't seen her in over a year."

"I'm sure it's nothing. We'll just ask her to stay the night and rest, especially after cooking like this." Monica opened up a container of whipped cream.

JD dipped his two fingers in. "Mmm...my favorite topping."

Monica grabbed his wrist. "Let me," she said then covered his fingers with her mouth and sucked them clean. She lifted a brow. "Now you no longer have to wonder what it's like to have your hand in my mouth."

JD's voice dropped and he pulled her to him. "I'll get you for that," he said then gave her mouth something else to do.

"Are you two coming?" Nadine called from the dining room.

Monica pulled away. "We'll be right there," she said as JD's mouth dipped to her neck.

"Tell her the pies are still cooling," he said, his breath hot against her skin.

Monica pushed him away. "They don't take *that* long to cool."

JD reluctantly released her and picked up a pie. "Fine." He briefly kissed her again. "And remember, I always finish what I've started."

Chapter 7

Night settled in slowly, taunting and teasing like a woman engaged in the dance of the seven veils—the sun turning the sky purple, pink, red and then a deep blue, letting the moon cast its radiant beams on the porch where they gathered. The scent of the recently eaten pies lingered in the air while the sound of crickets mingled in the cool, soft breeze. Monica stood in the doorway while JD sat on the porch railing and Nadine in an old wicker chair. Monica had made an excuse of having to find something so that she could give the pair some time alone. Before she left them she overheard Nadine complain about her appearance.

"I don't care what she says. I think she must be going blind, poor thing. I've never seen anyone so young having to wear big sunglasses all the time."

"Gran, she has sensitive eyes."

"And have you seen the way she dresses? At my

age I'm not really into fashion, but if she added some color and stopped wearing those darn rags on her head I think she could pretty herself up some. I even offered to pay for her to see my hairdresser, but she refused."

"I like her just the way she is."

"Don't tell me you're not a little curious."

"Oh, I'm curious, just not about the same things you are," JD said then changed the subject.

And Monica would have stayed away, busying herself in the kitchen so that they could converse in private, if he hadn't drawn her in with his music, which filtered through the open windows.

Monica knew he played the guitar, but she hadn't expected him to be a master. She felt mesmerized by each chord. It wasn't just an instrument but a voice singing a song about beauty, sorrow and loss. At first he played Eric Clapton's "Tears in Heaven" then effortlessly slipped into the Spanish guitar classic "Recuerdos de la Alhambra." Each note swept her away to Oklahoma and the house she'd grown up in before they'd moved East.

She remembered the expanse of land and being able to look up at the sky and see only stars with no buildings blocking the view, of horses grazing in the distance and riders racing past. She recalled the happy times visiting her aunt Corleen's house and eating fried bread while she told her stories and created jewelry to sell at the local roadside market for tourists. The music seemed to pull together pieces of her shattered soul and slowly glue them back together, reminding her of who she used to be.

"Stop hiding in the doorway and join us," Nadine said once JD had finished the song.

Monica stepped out onto the porch. "I wasn't hiding. I didn't want to disturb you." She looked at JD. "That was beautiful," she said as he put the guitar aside.

"Thank you." His words were simple but his gaze made her heart turn over.

"Has Monica shown you her studio?" Nadine asked.

"Yes," Monica cut in before JD could respond, remembering what had happened there.

"I was impressed," JD added.

Nadine nodded, pleased. "You should be. It's in your blood. Your heritage."

"Heritage?" Monica asked, confused.

JD shook his head, looking uncomfortable. "Gran, not now."

Nadine widened her eyes, amazed. "You mean he hasn't told you about his mother?"

Monica leaned forward, intrigued. "No."

JD picked up his guitar. "How would you two like another song?"

They both ignored him.

"She's a renowned jeweler," Nadine said to her captive audience. "As was her mother. Crystalline is an exceptional artist and is known for integrating precious stones with molded metals. Her work is still exhibited in some of the biggest art museums around the world. She's a natural. By the time she was in high school, she was making some of the most beautiful artwork seen by someone her age."

Monica turned to JD, stunned. "Crystalline is your mother?"

"Yes."

"Do you even know what his initials stand for?" Nadine continued.

"No, she doesn't," JD said in a cutting tone. "And she doesn't need to right now."

Nadine stopped, knowing that it wasn't wise to push her grandson too far. "I'm sure you'll tell her one day."

Monica stood, not knowing what to do with herself. He was related to Crystalline? She was a giant in the world of jewelry design. When he'd said he liked her work, was that pure flattery? Empty praise? "I can't believe you pretended to be so impressed with my little studio when your mother's work is internationally known."

"Monica, I wasn't pretending."

She paced, not hearing a word. "Making me put my little trinkets on when I've worn your—I mean, I've seen your mother's work worn on the most beautiful women in the world. Her gift makes my work seem like the efforts of a kindergartner."

JD grabbed her hand. "I may be a lot of things, but I'm not a liar. I don't flatter people to stroke their ego. I said I liked your work and I meant it. And I expected better than that from you. Now sit down."

Monica slowly sat, perplexed by his disappointment. "What do you mean?"

"Humility doesn't become you. You know you're good. You stay isolated in this little town selling your creations like they're dollar trinkets because you want to. Not because you have to."

That's where he was wrong. She didn't have a choice. "I'm still not in her league."

"You don't need to be. You're in your own. If you took some of my advice, I could turn you into an international sensation."

The thought made her shiver with anticipation. She could picture her work seen by millions, worn by VIPs around the globe, an enterprise based on her skills, not just her looks. But she couldn't risk the exposure.

She wanted to tell them about an aunt and a cousin who had taught her the art of making turquoise and silver jewelry. She wanted to share her background as a model, but she knew that she couldn't. "I don't want that."

JD pointed at her, his voice hard. "Then that's your choice. Don't put yourself down again."

"I won't."

"And never call me a liar."

"I didn't—" His harsh gaze stopped her words. "I won't." She glanced at her watch, eager to leave them. "It has been wonderful, but I really should get to bed." She stood and kissed Nadine on the cheek. "The extra room is all ready for you. See you in the morning."

"Good night," Nadine said then waited until Monica was gone before she looked at her grandson. "I'm so happy she's here. At first I wasn't sure I wanted to rent to her, but now I'm glad I did."

JD picked up his guitar and strummed a few chords then said, "What's really going on?"

Nadine tensed. "I don't—"

He shook his head, his voice becoming hard. "Don't lie to me. I know you too well. Your face is pale, you run out of energy easily…"

Nadine hung her head. "I'd hoped to keep it from you."

JD glanced away and sighed as though the weight of the world had fallen on him. "How long have you got?"

"A couple months."

He turned to her. "Have you gotten a second opinion?"

"A second, third and fourth." Nadine flashed a sad smile. "My time is running out."

"Why didn't you say anything? I could have had you seen by the best. I could have—"

His grandmother reached out and grabbed his hand. "I've lived a full life. It's okay."

JD shook his head. "Don't tell me that." He chewed his lower lip. "Are you in pain?"

"Some days are better than others." She squeezed his hand. "But I don't want to talk about me. Right now I'm happy and I want you to be happy too, and when I'm gone promise—"

JD stood, breaking her hold on him. "Don't ask me to promise anything. I failed my father and I'd fail you, too."

"You haven't failed, you just haven't realized that there's more to life than work and duty. Joy, love and happiness are not just words. They are real."

"Happiness," JD said, sounding out the word as if it were a curse. "Happiness in my life is always fleeting." He held up his hand before his grandmother could speak. "And it's nobody's fault. I'm not feeling sorry for myself. That's just the way it is, and I accept it. Whatever you want this summer, I'll do. You want a helicopter ride, I'll make it happen. You want a gourmet meal, a trip to Disney World, anything. Just let me know. But don't ask me for what I can't give you." He set his guitar aside and walked down the porch steps and into the dark night.

Nadine blinked back tears. "One day you will know that happiness can be yours."

He'd never felt so cold. JD returned to the still, quiet house, feeling numb. The warm breath of the summer evening couldn't pierce the chill that filled him. He felt nothing. He walked to the spare room where his grandmother slept and peeked his head inside. When he saw her sheets falling to the ground, he crept in and pulled them over her. He remembered how she and his father could laugh at anything. They could see the bright side of any sorrow. He hadn't gotten that gift. He remembered how she'd been there for him after his dad's funeral—plying him with good food, giving him errands so that he could feel important and leaving him alone when he didn't want to talk. Yes, she'd lived a full life, but she deserved a peaceful end, not the same one that had taken his father.

JD left her room and headed for his own, his legs feeling like lead. He felt old, worn. His Gran wasn't gone yet, but he already felt the weight of her loss. He stopped in front of his bedroom door and fumbled with the handle. Baxter pushed the door open and JD trudged after him, heading directly to his bed without turning on the lights. He collapsed on it, facedown, and waited for sleep.

"JD?"

He paused at the soft, almost mercurial voice, but he didn't move.

"JD?"

It sounded almost real and close. He lifted himself on his elbow and turned. He saw a female silhouette in the doorway, the hallway light behind her emphasizing her soft curves and ample figure. Every part of him came alert—painfully, like frozen limbs forced into hot water. He wanted her. Every part of him called out to her. He wanted her to come closer and share his bed, but all he said was, "Did I wake you?"

"No." Monica hesitated then stepped into the room, becoming part of the darkness. "I had my window open and heard what Nadine said. I'm sorry." She paused and studied him.

"Close the door and come here."

She quietly shut the door then crossed the room to him. "Yes?"

"You could have turned on the lights."

"I can still see you." She sat on the side of the bed. "You're shaking."

"It's nothing." He took her hand. "I just feel cold."

She began to stand. "I could make you some coffee or tea or—"

He pulled her down next to him. "No, you could do something else for me. Please," he whispered when he felt her stiffen. "I feel so cold. It's like something in me is dying and I want to feel alive again." He gathered her close. "Just warm me up a little."

Monica didn't hesitate. She wrapped her arms around his neck. "You are alive."

"Sometimes I wonder."

"You won't after tonight." She pulled off his shirt. "I'll keep you warm," she said, surprised by how cold he felt. It frightened her. His muscles felt hard and rigid, as if he were frozen. His lips that had once felt so soft were unyielding. She'd have to be careful, because he was on the abyss of shutting down both emotionally and physically. She knew it. She had felt it herself after Delong died and Anton had imprisoned her. Her limbs no longer felt as if they were her own. Her heart had solidified to stone. She couldn't feel anymore, but then she'd escaped and had learned to feel and live again, and she would help JD to do the same. She removed her robe and then her nightdress. "Touch me."

"I am."

Monica tried not to wince at the coolness of his fingers. She knew that would change soon. She saddled his waist then took a deep breath and set her glasses aside. "Kiss me."

He did. His bare chest pressing against her, his mouth hot and wet. She let him run his fingers through her long hair, slide them down her side and between her thighs. She felt his temperature rise, felt the silken sheen of sweat on his body. He reached for the side table.

Monica grabbed his hand. "No, no lights."

"Why not?"

"It's better this way."

"Oh, right. Your eyes."

"Yes."

"Okay." He pulled open the side drawer. "I've never wrapped him in the dark before."

"I can do it."

JD handed her a condom. "Please yourself."

"I plan to please you, too." Monica opened the package then groped for him in the dark.

"Um, that's my leg," he said with amusement.

"I know it's your leg."

"You're supposed to say you couldn't tell the difference."

"If you were that big I wouldn't be here." She rolled on the condom. "You're just the right size."

"Do you have night vision?"

"I don't need to see it to know."

JD laughed. "I wasn't talking about that. I mean can you see me, because I can sort of see you and you're absolutely beautiful."

"The moonlight helps."

"You don't need moonlight."

"I don't know about you, but I'm tired of this foreplay."

"You have a problem with compliments."

No, she'd been told she was beautiful before. It was nothing new, but she didn't want to tell him that so she grabbed his intimate part and said, "Do you need me to help guide you?"

"No, I can find my way."

"It's dark. I wouldn't want you to miss."

"I never miss. I'm as precise as a pilot landing on an airstrip, or a captain docking his ship."

"Your modesty is admirable," Monica said with a grin.

JD laughed then entered her as smoothly and expertly as he'd bragged he would. "Well done, Captain," Monica said. "Any passengers can now debark."

"Poor devils won't be getting far."

"But I can take you farther," she said, opening up and welcoming him deeper inside her. It was a snug, tight fit then he hit a spot that filled her with ecstasy. Their rhythmic motion made their shared desire rise to a frenzied passion. Like a tinderbox he caught fire from her flame. He was no longer cold, but hot, burning hot. She cried out his name, and they both sank into bliss. Afterward JD rolled away with a sigh of satisfaction.

Monica reached over and felt his forehead. "Good. The patient seems to be stabilized. You're no longer in danger of freezing and your temperature should soon return to normal."

"With you around I don't think it will ever be normal," he said with another long sigh.

Monica waited for the sound of his even breathing, a sign that he was asleep, then gathered her clothes and slipped out of his room.

Chapter 8

Monica woke up early the next morning and made a big breakfast of cinnamon waffles with eggs, bacon and a fruit salad to keep her mind from thinking about last night. Their night together had been explosive, risky and wonderful. It had taken her hours to get to sleep that night and when she finally did, she did so with a smile. But now it was morning and she wasn't sure what she would say to him.

"I thought you might like seeing one of Crystalline's designs," Nadine said, coming into the kitchen with a magazine folded to a specific page.

"I've seen them."

Nadine dismissed her statement and placed the magazine on the counter. "I bet you haven't seen this."

Monica turned and nearly choked. It was a close-up picture of her—as Venus—dressed in a green silk kimono and emerging from the water with a large pendant draped around her neck. One sleeve hung loosely off her shoulder as she stared straight into the camera in a seductive pose. Fortunately, Nadine didn't seem to sense her surprise and continued talking. "This was one of her happiest moments. She was over the moon when Venus wore her necklace."

"Venus wore what?" JD asked, coming into the kitchen. "Mmm...something smells good."

"Cinnamon waffles," Monica said, trying to divert his attention when he went over to look at the magazine.

"Good. I hope you're making enough."

Nadine tapped the picture. "I was just showing Monica one of your mother's greatest accomplishments."

JD looked at the picture, but Monica couldn't guess whether he was studying the jewelry or the woman.

"Most of it's probably airbrushed," Monica said, unnerved by his interest.

"I heard that Venus was all real," JD said. "Definitely looks like it. Shame she's disappeared."

"Probably still mourning her husband's death," Nadine said. "I understand. When I lost my Walter it was hard. But I'm sure it's even harder for her."

"How come?"

"Rumor has it that Delong Price was her creator and the only reason she existed."

Monica held back a groan. Was that what people thought? They thought that she was nothing without Delong? That he'd created her as he did his sculptures and paintings? She wanted to tell them that she'd also had a hand in her success. That it wasn't just luck or her husband, but hard work and strategy that had helped her reach the top of her field. She'd created Venus, too. But she knew she couldn't defend herself, so she snatched the magazine and closed it. "Breakfast is ready. Let's eat," she said, eager to change the subject.

To her annoyance, Nadine refused to let it go. As they sat at the breakfast table she said, "You dated her once, didn't you, JD?"

"Dated who?" JD asked, scooping up some fruit salad.

"Venus."

"You think I dated Venus? No way. I don't date models."

"Venus was more than just a model," Monica said, unable to keep silent.

Nadine nodded as she poured syrup on her cinnamon waffles "She's right. Venus was an icon. And don't play dumb. You've dated models before."

JD shook his head. "No, I haven't and I don't. It's a rule of mine."

"Why?" Monica asked.

"They're not my type."

"What about that one from South Africa?" Nadine interjected. "You were seeing her."

He nodded. "But I wasn't dating her."

"What were you doing with her then?"

He grinned.

Nadine shook her head. "You naughty boy."

His grin grew.

"You should behave." She sent Monica a nervous glance. "You're giving Monica the wrong impression of you."

JD sent Monica a significant look. "I doubt it. I think Monica knows me pretty well by now."

Monica narrowed her eyes but didn't reply. If he mentioned last night in front of Nadine, she would hurt him. Badly.

"Isn't that right?" he continued with a smile, as if daring her to challenge him, then took a bite of the waffle.

Nadine set her drink down. "Don't tease her."

"I'd never do that," JD said then placed his hand on Monica's lap.

She lifted a knife in warning; he only slid his hand farther down.

Nadine sighed with joy. "This house feels so wonderful again with you two in it. You bring a special energy."

"Yes, real special," JD said then squeezed Monica's thigh. He removed his hand before she could prick him with her knife. He took it from her.

"What is it about women and knives?"

"You should know."

Nadine introduced a new topic and they resumed breakfast in ease and good humor. JD clapped his hands together once he was done and said, "So, Gran, where would you like me to take you today?"

"I just want to sit and read and then take a nap, but there's something you two can do for me."

"Okay," he said with some hesitation.

"I want you to go to the craft fair and buy me three things—a guitar stand, a rocking chair and a handmade knotted rug, and I want you to set them in the family room."

JD frowned. "We can wait until after your nap and you can come with us. I know how much you like to shop."

Nadine shook her head. "I want you to buy them for me as a gift."

Monica's voice cracked with a shade of panic. "But I can't—"

"No problem," JD interrupted with a shrug. "We'll do it." He left to get his wallet and keys.

Monica started to follow, but Nadine grabbed her hand. "When you get him to tell you what his initials mean you'll break through his wall."

"I doubt I'll ever get him to share those kinds of secrets with me, and I can't—"

"Try," Nadine said with a strange urgency. "Please."

Monica nodded her head.

"And don't worry about me. I have Baxter to keep me company."

"I can't go," Monica said when JD returned. Nadine had gone to lie down in her bedroom.

"Why not?"

Monica wrung her hands like a nervous child. "I just can't."

"That's not an answer."

"I don't do well in crowds."

JD grinned. "Don't worry. I'll protect you."

"I'm serious."

His grin faded. "So am I." He took her hand. "You have nothing to be afraid of. Come on."

Monica still held back. "But JD, I—"

"Is it a phobia?"

"No. It's just that crowds make me nervous."

He lowered his voice. "I'll keep you close the whole time. You have nothing to fear. Trust me. Okay?"

Monica swallowed and nodded her head. For a moment she wanted to tell him everything. Why she was hiding. Why she avoided people. Why she couldn't be seen. But she just nodded and pushed down her anxiety. He was right. She had nothing to worry about. Nobody knew her and no one would be paying attention to her. She was sure Anton couldn't find her here. She took a deep breath. "I'm fine."

"Of course, it would help if you told me what—or rather, who—you were afraid of."

"No personal questions, remember?"

He sighed. "Yes. Let's go. It shouldn't take us too long to find what Gran wants."

It took them over two hours. The fair buzzed with numerous stalls boasting a wide assortment of vendors trying to sell their wares. In addition to the regular handcrafted items there were those unusual items like old maps and crystal chandeliers that got the attention of shoppers and other onlookers. One vendor was selling a set of coasters made out of pieces of bark, which interested Monica, until she overheard him describe using cow dung to hold the items together and then shellacking them.

And there was the woman who crocheted every item in her stall from earrings and necklaces to thong panties.

"Things have definitely changed," JD said, looking at a bright red set. He glanced at Monica with renewed interest.

She shook her head. "Don't even think about it."

"How about the purple one?"

"No."

He laughed and rested his arms around her shoulders. "Worth a try." They walked at a leisurely pace through the crush of people, the loud voices and scent of spicy seafood and sweet candy floss.

Monica felt on edge. As Venus she could make crowds part and make men mute. She knew her beauty was both powerful and dangerous. But as Monica she wasn't sure how to handle herself. She wanted to blend in with the crowd, but that was impossible with JD. Not because of anything he did, but because of the type of man he was. His confident, magnetic presence drew stares from women, men and children. Twice she tried to distance herself, offering to look for one item while he searched for another, but he stayed stubbornly by her side.

"You might leave me alone in bed," he said at her second attempt to sneak away, "but you're not leaving me alone here."

"You were sleeping soundly."

"Because I dreamed of waking up to you."

"That won't happen."

"Why not?"

"That's just the way it has to be. I like sleeping in my own bed by myself. It's just a preference."

He tenderly caressed her cheek with his finger. "My Cinderella girl. The clock strikes midnight and you disappear." He halted. "I see some rocking chairs," he said and led her to the vendor's stand before she could protest. JD's acceptance of her behavior made her feel more relaxed. She thought he might try to persuade her or get angry, but he'd done neither. She felt her uneasiness dissipate. Everyone else fell away and she focused on him. She liked being with him, being in his presence. She felt safe and cherished.

Monica took a deep breath and wiggled her shoulders, feeling all tension go. She could be ordinary. No one would stop her for a photograph or an autograph. No one gawked or stared. She helped JD select a rocker and then they rewarded themselves with baked pretzels and hot mustard.

It would have been the perfect afternoon, if she hadn't seen them.

Chapter 9

Monica stopped in front of a row of hand-painted por-
celain dolls lined up in glass compartments. Their wide,
sightless eyes stared back at her. That's what Anton had
called them: his dolls. He'd kept them like a collection,
and for over three months she'd been part of it...

"Careful, you're still a little groggy," a deep, cultured
male voice had said.

Monica held her head to keep the room from spinning. She remembered eating dinner with her husband's
friend Anton Stevens—a man she'd never really liked
but tolerated. He'd come over to her house to console
her and she'd let him in, although his visit was unexpected. Most of her staff was gone because she'd given
them a holiday. She didn't want anyone around. Her
personal chef had left her food to reheat, but she didn't
have an appetite for anything.

But Anton arrived on her doorstep and persuaded her

to dine with him by saying that he was worried about her and that she shouldn't be alone. She accepted his invitation because she was eager for the company of someone who knew Delong as well as she did. Since she couldn't get support from her sister, Anton seemed the next-best thing. He had been a big supporter of Delong's work and a friend for many years. He'd never married but lived an active lifestyle, although she never saw him with a woman.

She'd once suspected he was gay, but Delong had laughed at the idea and said that Anton just liked to keep his private life private. He wasn't in the closet. Unlike other men, he never tried to flirt with her and kept her at arm's length. She didn't care because he was older and Delong's friend, not hers. But that night he was a welcome presence. He had a sumptuous meal delivered and they ate on the balcony. She remembered the taste of sautéed potatoes and crisp asparagus spears, but that was all.

Now her mind felt fuzzy, her throat dry and her mouth pasty. She squinted at the unfamiliar gilded room around her. She slowly sat up and saw she was on a large, ornate bed with a canopy. "Where am I?"

"With me," Anton said from the foot of the bed. "Where you're meant to be."

She wasn't in the mood for riddles. "Please take me home."

"You are home."

Monica sat up straighter. "Stop playing games, Anton. I'm tired and I want to go home."

"You are home," he said in the same cool tone. "You're staying with me from now on."

Monica swung her feet over the side of the bed and stood. "No, I'm not." She walked toward the door and promptly fell on the ground. She turned and saw her ankle gripped in a pair of leg irons attached to a post.

Anton stood over her. "I had to take some precautions to make sure you don't try to do anything foolish like run away. If you behave yourself, we'll remove them." He held out his hand to help her up.

She glared at him and stood on her own. "You can't keep me here."

Her anger didn't faze him. "Change is always an adjustment, but you'll get used to it."

"I'm not staying here."

He touched her face; she yanked back. "I always love breaking in the feisty ones." He seized her throat and his voice turned hard. "You can't escape from me." He released her and smiled. "But you won't be the first to try," he said then left.

It was a joke. It had to be. He couldn't think he could keep her here. But Delong did have some odd friends with strange eccentricities. Perhaps Anton felt a need to protect her because she was on her own. Some feared she might even contemplate suicide because Delong had made up so much of her world. But he didn't need to worry. She didn't need to be kept here and watched. She'd let him know that and then everything would be fine.

She waited for him to return, but he didn't. Not that night anyway. Instead a woman in a stylish West African wrap dress scurried into the room. Her braided hair was swept to the top of her head, and her eyes were large and brown. She had a large scar down one side of her face and on her neck, but that didn't hide the fact that she'd once been beautiful.

"Could you get Anton for me?" Monica asked the woman.

She shook her head.

"Can you tell me where I am?"

The woman shook her head again then pressed her fingers against her lips.

"You can't talk at all?"

She nodded.

Monica sighed. She would have to find someone else to get her questions answered. The tiny woman moisturized Monica's skin and then helped her into a new dress. Just as quickly as she'd entered the room, she left, and Monica sat on the bed and waited. Moments later two men showed up with guns.

"Stand up," one said while the other marched toward her. He unlatched her leg irons and gently shoved her forward. "Go."

The sight of the guns changed everything. Anton was more than eccentric—he was dangerous and he wasn't a man she could trust. She wouldn't be able to reason with him. She had to escape him.

Monica left the room sandwiched between the two guards. As she strolled down the long hallway, she could tell by the height of the walls that it was an enormous structure, but she didn't let that deter her. When she saw a window, she knew what she had to do. She'd taken a self-defense course after a gang had assaulted Delong and her as they were walking from a gala event in an attempt to kidnap her. She'd gotten free from them, terrified and shaken and determined not to feel that helpless again. She'd learned to shoot and to fight. She would put those fighting skills to use now.

Monica pretended to trip, which startled the guard behind her, giving her enough time to jab him in the neck with her elbow. The other guard spun around and she kneed him, grabbed his gun and butted him with it then ran to the window. It was locked. She raced down the hall just as one of the guards sounded an alarm. She couldn't find an exit. One hall led to another and then another, like a labyrinth.

She ran down one way and reached a wall.

"Venus, there's no need for this."

She spun around and saw Anton with five guards behind him.

"You might as well kill me now."

"Why would I want to do that? I adore you."

"Where am I?"

"You're home." He made a gesture with his hand and the guards rushed her. She tried to fight them off, but they anticipated her every move. She felt a needle prick and then nothing.

Monica woke in the same gilded room hours later. She was kept there for the next several days. Except for the silent woman who helped change her outfits and brought her food, she didn't see anyone else. Monica had to escape. She suspected they were putting something in her food to keep her drowsy, so she ate only the raw vegetables and dumped the rest, and soon her mind became clear. Whenever the guards or the mystery woman were around, she pretended to be docile and quiet so they wouldn't suspect anything.

After another week she was released from her solitude and allowed to eat in the main dining hall. It was an elaborate ballroom with gold table settings, silk furnishings and marble pillars. There she saw sixteen other beautiful women, from all parts of the world, some who seemed listless and uninterested in their surroundings.

Anton sat at the head of the long table. Monica sat down, trying not to look too alert, and quickly learned that they were not allowed to talk to each other. She stared down at her food.

"Don't have an appetite, Venus?"

She couldn't let him suspect that she had every reason to be suspicious. She took a large spoonful.

"Good. Eat up, my darlings."

Venus kept her head lowered throughout dinner and then she was led back to her room. For the next month she followed the rules and was given more privileges. She was allowed to sit out in the garden with another woman from Korea. The guardians, as she'd learned to call them, were always close by, but as long as they walked slowly and didn't talk too long, "the dolls" were allowed to converse with each other.

She caught the other woman's eye and the woman pretended to tie her shoe while Monica studied a flower.

"How long have you been here?" she asked her.

"Six months, but I'm luckier than some. I'm a side project."

"What's that?"

"I'm just here for his pleasure. He's involved in the sex trade and sells women like produce. He keeps the ones he wants for his private entertainment. The ones he really wants to control he keeps sedated. Some get addicted, I'm told. He just got rid of a huge shipment, which is why there are only sixteen of us."

So that explained some of the women and others who couldn't seem to keep still and seemed jittery and anxious. Fortunately, she had avoided that fate. "We have to find a way out."

"There isn't one. No one has ever escaped. One woman tried to escape and broke her nose and several bones in her face when she fell into one of the many traps found on the estate. They found her, and a week later she disappeared. Another girl took a knife to her face and other parts of her body, hoping that if she disfigured herself he wouldn't want her and would let her go. He took her somewhere, and she came back so terrified she hasn't said a word since and is forced to take care of us."

"You mean Lola?" Monica asked, astonished, referring to the quiet woman who dressed her.

"Yes. It's hopeless. No one knows we're here because he chooses women either estranged from their families or alone. Oh, no. A guard is getting suspicious." The woman stood and walked away.

Monica gripped her fist. Death was worth the risk. It was a better choice than being a prisoner. She tried to connect with the others, but her talk of escape frightened them and soon everyone avoided her. So most days she wandered the compound alone and becoming more discouraged. All of that changed the night Felicia Hightower was brought to the compound.

Monica was walking past Anton's "market room," where he entertained mostly men and showed off his collection. She hadn't been shown off yet but had overheard from others what the experience was like. He also received new women there. Today was one of those days.

Felicia was a petite woman, about five feet, a breath-taking beauty with a short-cropped afro and a figure most women would starve for and most men would lust after. Her smooth ebony skin, turned-up nose and rose-bud lips were made complete by a pair of large almond-shaped eyes, expertly outlined with a blue liner. Monica found herself unable to stop staring at the young woman sitting stubbornly erect on a wicker stool as one of the guardians attached her, by a leg chain, to a nearby post.

Her face was tear-stained but did not hide a sense of determination. From what Monica could see there seemed to be a small bruise on the side of her face. This fact was confirmed when she overheard Anton berating one of the guardians.

"I gave strict orders. My merchandise is always to be delivered untouched."

"She tried to escape and I had to…"

"You had to what?"

The guardian fell silent.

"Get rid of her. I don't want damaged goods. You will not receive payment until she is replaced."

"Yes, sir."

Monica ducked out of sight when the guardian led the new arrival to the holding room. Monica's heart skipped a beat. Get rid of her? Monica knew she could not sit by and do nothing. Felicia would be her means of escape.

That night she called on the strength of her ancestor who Monica felt inhabited her.

Her great-great-grandmother had been abducted from her tribe at an early age. She did not remember being taken, but as she grew, she knew she was not like the others. While the members of her tribe had dark-tanned skin, with thick coarse hair and broad features, she was light-skinned, with fine black hair. Her fine features made her a focus of envy and lust, and to prevent her from being stolen, she was forced to stay hidden from sight. Like Monica, she was not allowed to do what other children did.

While she watched the other girls work all day getting water, helping clean the hides and gathering wood for the fire, she was taught how to make baskets, pottery and jewelry. As she grew, her great-great-grandmother developed her skills and became known for her expertly crafted jewelry, which was eventually displayed in prominent museums, including the renowned Smithsonian Institution's National Museum of the American Indian. And while creating jewelry, she had learned about compounds and poisons. This knowledge became useful when an enemy tribe threatened to take their land and steal all the women and children.

With the agreement of the chief, her great-great-grandmother helped come up with a compound that they put into the enemy tribe's drinking water. And while the men slept, they were slaughtered. The women and children, as was the case during warfare, were then taken captive by her tribe.

The carnage had frightened her great-great-grandmother, and she'd stayed away from poisons after that. But everything changed when her eldest daughter needed to escape her abusive husband. She created a compound that left him sexually ineffective, and he left her in shame. She then taught her daughters the power of specific plants, just in case they needed them. "Respect the land, for she protects you," she liked to say. "And she'll save you like no man can." As Monica thought, an idea grew in her mind.

"You're a brave woman," she said to Lola the next day.

"And I need you to do a brave thing for me." She slipped her a list. "Get these items. I don't care how, but I need them by tonight."

Lola took the list and nodded. After dinner Monica returned to her room and found the items tucked under her pillow. She had one part of her plan down; now, on to the next. That night she crept into the holding room and whispered to Felicia, "I need you to trust me." She slipped the packet under the door. "In two minutes I want you to scream then swallow the contents of this packet and stuff the empty packet in your bra."

"But—"

"There's no time to explain. I want to save your life." *And mine.*

"Okay," Felicia said with the determination Monica had first seen in her.

Monica hid behind a large broad-leaved plant and waited. Felicia did as told, and the alarm sounded and two guardians rushed into the room.

One swore. "She's dead."

"What do you mean?"

"Check her pulse. She doesn't have one."

"Stevens can't know about this."

"He was going to get rid of her anyway."

"Damn, I'd wanted to have a crack at her."

"I'll go get the van. Dump her in the box," he said, referring to the large rectangular box they used to get rid of girls who died from overdoses or other reasons. "We might as well clean this mess up tonight."

One guard left and she heard the other lifting Felicia into the box. Then she saw Lola come and wave to the guard to get his attention and hand him a note. "What now?"

She nodded.

He glanced at the box, clearly conflicted, then said, "All right, show me what you need, but make it quick." He followed Lola. Monica snuck inside the room and climbed in the box with Felicia, who wasn't dead but was in a catatonic state from the compound she'd given her. She'd come out of it in a few hours.

Monica heard the footsteps of the guardians return and felt herself being lifted.

"Damn, she's heavy," one grunted.

"Dead weight always is. Now shut up and go."

Minutes later Monica felt the box being lifted onto a truck, and soon she was out of the compound and on the road to freedom.

"Monica?"

JD's voice cut through her thoughts, and she turned to see his worried face. She was free. This was a man who didn't want to possess her. This was a man who didn't need to own her. With him she was still her own woman. She remembered him selecting the perfect rocking chair for his grandmother. His attention to detail and concern that it not tilt back too far. She knew he was a man she could love. A man she already loved. Not that he needed to know that. With him she was safe. Her secret was safe, and soon she would go back to the farmhouse and the new life she'd created for herself. She took JD's hand and smiled. "I'm all right. I was just enjoying this perfect day."

They returned to the house in the early evening, just as the sun lengthened the shadows.

"I know just the place where I'm going to put this," JD said as he untied the rocking chair from the top of the car. "I'm going to put it near the fireplace where Gran can keep warm and work on her crocheting."

Monica looked at him, surprised. "She crochets?"

"No, but she's always wanted to learn." And he'd help her before it was too late, JD thought with sudden determination. Maybe the doctors were wrong. Maybe if he stayed longer and made the place comfortable she could get better. Life in town wasn't good for her. She belonged at the farmhouse. She needed to be near the trees and land she loved. He turned to look at Monica take out the knotted rug from the car, and he remembered how she'd selected just the one she thought would be perfect for Gran. She'd grown to love her as much as he did. He could feel the bond between them. He looked at the house and welcomed its presence. He would fill it with all that his grandmother wanted, and maybe he could be happy. Tonight, anything seemed possible.

Monica held the front door open for him, and Baxter greeted them at the door with a little yelp.

"Nice to see you, too," JD said as he headed to the family room. Baxter followed him and yelped again.

"I think something's wrong," Monica said. "It's not like Baxter to bark."

JD set the rocking chair down. "He's just excited to see us," he said, wanting to dismiss the eerie silence and Baxter's strange behavior. "Gran, we're back," he called out. "And I think you're going to like what we got you."

He walked into the family room and found Nadine lying facedown on the couch. JD rushed over to her and knelt by her side, turning her face to him. "Gran?" He touched her forehead. Her skin felt pasty and damp. He took her hand and warmed it between his. "Gran, honey?"

Her eyes fluttered open. "I'm so glad you're here," she said in a weak voice.

Monica rushed over to the phone. "I'm calling the ambulance."

"Won't do any good," Nadine wheezed.

"Don't say things like that," JD said. "You're going to be fine." He stood. "Let me—"

"No, just stay with me."

JD fell to his knees, feeling helpless while Monica dialed. "Gran, let me get you some juice and a blanket. I can carry you to your room."

Nadine shook her head. "Did you get the items?"

"Does it matter?" he snapped.

"Yes, we got them," Monica said in a softer tone then returned to her conversation with the emergency operator.

"Good," Nadine said. "I'm so glad I got to see you again."

JD shook his head, trying his best not to lose his

temper. He wouldn't let the evening end like this. He'd get her to the hospital and she'd be fine. "Don't talk. Just save your strength."

"Promise me one thing."

"Gran, I told you—"

"Be happy, JD. That's all we've ever wanted for you."

It was his father all over again. It was a cruel irony that, just like in the past, he couldn't promise her that one thing. But unlike the boy he'd been when his father had died, he was able to control his feelings and push down his anger and sadness and kiss the back of her hand. When he spoke, his voice was calm. "Just rest, Gran. I promise I'll never leave your side."

Chapter 10

Nadine passed away a week later. There were moments when the doctors thought she would rally, but she slipped quietly into a coma from which she never recovered, and then one day her heart stopped. Her physician admitted to JD that she was sicker than she let anyone know.

At the repast, which was held in the farmhouse she loved, Monica kept herself busy in the kitchen, making sure the catering was on schedule. Being in the kitchen allowed her to feel useful. Even though she'd loved Nadine, she felt like an outsider among her family and friends. Also, she didn't want to think about what Nadine's death meant for her future. She'd have to find a new place to live. Whoever inherited the farmhouse, even if it was JD, might want to move in right away or sell it. She couldn't buy it. Not right now. The paper trail was too dangerous.

It was probably better this way. She was getting too attached to the place and JD. It was time to move on.

JD peeked his head in. "I thought I'd find you here."

"I just—"

"You're a guest, not the waitstaff," JD said, taking Monica's hand. "Come on." He pulled her into the other room then handed her a glass. "Relax, Monica."

A man suddenly turned around and grinned. He was a tad shorter and lighter-skinned than JD, but he had his smile and a wicked gleam in his eye. "Did I hear you say Monica, big brother? At last I get to meet the sexy artist you've been telling me about."

JD made the introductions. "This is my brother, Donnie. Donnie, this is Monica."

Donnie couldn't hide his surprise as he stared at Monica then he burst into laughter. "This is a joke, right? Good one, bro." He playfully punched JD in the arm. "You almost got me. Really. Where is she?"

JD lowered his voice, his eyes blazing. "She's right in front of you."

Donnie's smile fell and his face turned crimson. "You're serious?"

JD's eyes darkened as he folded his arms.

His younger brother swore. "I didn't mean to—"

Monica waved his embarrassment aside, even though she felt mortified herself. "It's okay." She took a step back. "I have to tell the caterer something. Excuse me." She slipped out of JD's grasp when he reached for her and weaved her way through the crowd, desperate to escape to her room. She didn't make it. A stunning woman blocked her path. She was impeccably dressed in a black silk designer pantsuit and a pair of three-inch

Italian leather pumps, and she was wearing a magnificent mother-of-pearl necklace with matching earrings. Although Monica was several inches taller, the other woman carried herself as if they were of equal height.

She had smooth dark skin and piercing eyes, which were outlined with a deep purple kohl pencil. Her other features were softer. Monica could not help noticing how striking this woman looked. There was something about her that kept Monica entranced. Crystalline had that affect on people.

"I'd like a word with you," JD's mother said. Her hair was swept up in a chignon, giving her the look of a living sculpture. Monica had seen her at the funeral service but hadn't spoken to her. Now she followed her over to a corner.

"My son tells me you make jewelry."

"Yes, but I'm nowhere in your league. You're a true artisan and I have always—"

Crystalline held up her hand. "Save the flattery, please. That's not why I want to talk to you. My son has taken a keen interest in you."

"I like him, too."

"Most women do, for one reason or another."

Monica stiffened. "My reasons are pure."

Crystalline paused. "I've met a lot of people, but only once have I ever met near perfection. Unlike others, I notice things like the shape of one's forehead to the ratio of one's neck or shoulders. Few people have the perfect elongated neck that makes jewelry shine. I saw that once when I met Venus. You may have heard about her, or seen her picture. Over the past ten years she was featured in every major magazine." She looked straight into Monica's face as if she could see past the shield of her sunglasses. "I saw it again. Today, when I saw you. Your attempt at dressing down didn't fool me. I'd know your profile if you were covered in feathers."

"I—"

"I don't know what game you're playing, but I won't allow anyone to toy with my son."

"Don't worry. I wouldn't do anything to hurt him. I'll be gone after tonight."

Crystalline looked as if she wanted to take her up on the offer, but she suddenly shook her head. "He won't let you."

"I'm my own woman."

She rested a hand on her hip and considered Monica. "Then why are you hiding?"

"It's complicated, but please—"

"I won't say a word. I'm an expert when it comes to secrets. No one will hear anything from me." She looked up and saw JD. "As long as you don't give me a reason to."

"I won't," Monica promised then left and went into the extra room where Nadine had stayed. She pulled off the quilt that covered the bed and wrapped herself in it then sat on the floor, feeling as if she was in her own cocoon. She closed her eyes, just wanting everything to stop. She wanted Nadine to be alive again, to have never met JD's mother, to have never met JD. Everything would have been different if he hadn't entered her life.

Look after him for me. Monica heard Nadine's words echoing in her mind. But who would look out for her? She thought of the loss of her husband and her old life and then the loss of the new life she'd created. She hung her head and cried. She wept until her chest ached and her throat was sore then lay on the ground and covered herself with the quilt, blocking out the world.

Monica woke up hours later, shocked when she saw the clock. It said 9 a.m. She'd slept nearly twelve hours. She hadn't realized she was so exhausted. She replaced the quilt then returned to her room. She changed out of the clothes she had slept in and jumped in the shower. She didn't stay long. She knew JD was leaving that morning. He hadn't said a word, but he didn't need to. His vacation had come to an end. She went downstairs and noticed his suitcase by the door.

"Are you all ready to go?" Monica said when JD entered the kitchen a few minutes later. She took care to keep her voice neutral.

"Yes. I just came back from dropping Baxter at the shelter. I donated a large sum of money and gave instructions that he's not to be put down but worked with until he's ready for a new family."

Another loss. She'd no longer see Baxter chewing on his favorite doggie bone, jumping at shadows or greeting her at the door wagging his tail so hard his entire back end shook. Monica felt her heart softly crack. "I see." She cleared her throat. "Well, have a safe trip."

"Monica—"

She went to the kitchen cabinet and pulled down a plate and glass. "You have to go. I understand that. It hasn't been the quiet vacation you'd hoped for."

JD walked up behind her and turned her to face him. "That night with you was wonderful. And although…" He sighed and struggled for words. "I don't regret a thing about coming here. What happened when we were together—"

"Is over."

"It doesn't have to be." He hesitated. "My life in the city is complicated, but it's simple here and I like it that way. I can't make you any promises. I want to see you again without any strings. I won't put any pressure on you, and you'll do the same. I won't ask you why you're here, and you won't ask what I do when I'm away from you. We'll just meet on holidays for times like these. What do you say?"

"I don't know if I'll still be here. I have to find another place and—"

JD rested his hands on her shoulders. "You don't have to go anywhere. The place is mine. Gran gave it to me with specific instructions that you stay for as long as you like."

The tightness in her chest began to ease. She didn't have to leave. She would be safe here. "Nadine was always so generous."

"You haven't answered my question."

Monica bit her lip. No strings attached. No questions. No promises. She'd see him only on holidays. Yes, that could work. It meant that it wasn't anything serious and his mother wouldn't have to worry. "No one would know?"

He shrugged. "No one needs to. What I do is no one's business."

She licked her lips. "Okay."

He grinned. "Good. I have time off for Thanksgiving, unless you have family that you want to see then."

Monica quickly shook her head. "No, I'll be here."

"Okay, I'll see you then." He kissed her then pulled away and left without looking back. As he drove away Monica realized he hadn't said goodbye.

"Let her go? Did you just say I should let her go?"

Gerald held the phone away from his ear. Even though Stevens wasn't shouting, his cool delivery was just as effective. "It's just a suggestion."

"You may be the best in the business, but you can and will be replaced. Can you do the job or not?"

"Of course. It's just getting expensive." Finding Venus had taken a lot longer than he'd anticipated.

"That's my problem, not yours. Any developments?"

"She's definitely in the U.S., and that's all I'll say for now." He hung up. Gerald knew he'd taken a risk by advising Stevens to forget about Venus, but he'd been willing to take the gamble because part of him liked her. Part of him liked how cunning she was. She'd outsmarted Stevens and was giving Gerald a hard time. As each day passed he'd become more impressed with her fortitude, her false leads and misdirection. He remembered when she was in the limelight. God, he could imagine just one night with her. But now he knew there was a keen mind behind that beauty.

She deserved a free pass, but he wasn't the boss. If Stevens was willing to pay to find her, then it was fine with him.

His cell phone rang just as he lay down for a nap. He swore. If it was Stevens again, he was going to up his price. "Hicks."

"I've got a job for you," a low familiar voice said.

"Sorry, I've already got an assignment."

"This one won't take you long." When the voice told him the target, Gerald sat up with interest. "Is this some kind of joke?"

"No, it's a family thing." The voice told him the amount they were willing to offer then said, "Think about it." Then the line went dead.

Gerald rested against the headboard. He'd never worked on two cases before, but Venus made locating the second target easy. The woman wasn't only a goddess but a sorceress. She could make him a very rich man. It was a risk, but he'd never liked playing it too safe. He brought up Venus's image on his phone and gazed longingly at it. The woman was so hot—dressed in skintight jeans and a tank top—he was surprised the phone didn't melt in his hand. "I'll find you, Venus," he said to the image. "And it will be a pleasure."

Over the next few weeks Monica busied herself with work. But she couldn't stop thinking about JD and Nadine. She'd come here to be alone, away from people, and two had already stolen her heart. She worked on new jewelry designs and patrolled the woods to make sure that Drent and his crew hadn't come back. Everything seemed to settle back to normal then one day as she cleaned the foyer, she heard scratching on the front door. She opened it and saw Baxter.

He sauntered past her, as if he was where he was meant to be, leaving dirty paw prints on her newly swept floor.

"Come back here."

He turned to her and wagged his tail. He looked as though he'd traveled for days; his fur held grass stains and stray leaves and was caked down with dirt and mud.

Monica bent down to stroke him then changed her mind. "You bad boy. What are you doing here?"

He licked her hand.

That melted her heart. She picked him up and hugged him. "I missed you, too." She set him back down and shook her head, wondering what she should do next.

"JD's not here and they're going to be looking for you…but let me clean you up first."

Monica washed and fed him then picked up the phone.

"Thank God!" the shelter coordinator said when Monica explained the situation. "We just took them out for exercise and he jumped the fence and ran! We've been searching for days."

Monica looked at Baxter and made a decision. The determined little dog deserved a permanent home. "I'll keep him." When JD returned he could formerly adopt him, and she'd look after him when JD was out of town.

The coordinator agreed with Monica's plan and everything was settled. Monica smiled. She knew when JD came back he'd be in for a big surprise.

But as summer turned to fall, touching the leaves with yellow, crimson and amber, Monica wasn't sure JD would return. She sensed that the farm held too many memories. Sad ones that hurt: the rocking chair that sat in the corner unused; the guitar stand that stood empty while the guitar was sealed up in a case inside the closet; and the knotted rug that lay discarded on the family room floor. Once he was back in the city he'd get accustomed to its fast pace and excitement and would forget her, which was exactly what she needed. One of them had to be sensible. It had been a fantastic, hot love affair, and after two months she couldn't see how it could continue the way it had been. Would he really want to see her again, just for a night in bed?

Monica continued to doubt JD's return, but as Thanksgiving drew near she held out hope even at the risk of being disappointed. Two days before the holiday she scrubbed down the walls in the kitchen and dining room and purchased a festive orange table cloth, an elegant place setting, and a vase of fresh flowers as the centerpiece. On Thanksgiving Day, Monica spent all day preparing a feast. She made a sweet potato casserole, three-bean salad, fried green tomatoes (she learned how to cook them because JD had once mentioned they were his favorite food), roasted turkey with corn bread dressing and, for dessert, a homemade blackberry cobbler and apricot cookie rolls.

After that she took a long, hot shower and lathered herself in expensive creams and oil then put on a layered tunic-like soft pink dress with a silk head wrap and waited.

And waited.

And waited.

And he didn't come.

Chapter 11

"What do you mean he's in jail?"

"JD," his mother said in a tart voice. "You know I hate it when you shout."

"What is Donnie doing in jail?" JD asked, trying to keep rein on his temper.

"He got into a little trouble, that's all."

"He always gets into a little trouble."

"I'm sure that once you bail him out, everything will be cleared."

JD released a fierce sigh. "Fine, where is he?" He could drop by the jail, pay the fee and still make it to the farmhouse.

"Nevada."

JD paused. "I'm sorry, did you say Nevada?"

"Yes."

"What the hell is he doing there?"

"JD, you're shouting again."

He lowered his voice. "Answer my question."

"It's complicated. He told me it was a business deal. We can't just leave him in jail over the holiday weekend."

Yes, we can. "I have plans."

"Really?"

"Yes," he said, annoyed by his mother's surprise.

"You know I would go, but these situations are always so stressful for me. You're so good with him, and you always were. You could get there in no time. Denis said he'd let you use his private jet. He still doesn't know why you won't get one of your own."

"Since he's so concerned, why doesn't he go?" JD asked, referring to his mother's present boyfriend.

"He's here with me. His daughter made a special dinner, and—"

Right. It seemed that everyone else's holiday plans mattered more than his. Probably because he'd never had any before. Usually he was at work and could rescue his brother at a moment's notice. It would annoy him, but it usually didn't bother him this much. This time he had spent weeks thinking about Monica and what they would do when he saw her again. And he would see her again. Nothing would stop that. He could make a phone call and have someone else handle it, but he didn't like to use his staff for his personal life. He glanced at his watch, weighing his options. If he scheduled everything right, he could still make it to Monica. He picked up his phone.

Monica stared at the ringing phone, not sure if she wanted to answer. What excuse would he give her?

Would he say that work got busy, that he'd forgotten and wanted to take a rain check, that he'd met someone else? Why even call at all? Soon the ringing stopped and she regretted letting her imagination run wild with different scenarios instead of hearing his explanation. What if he was just delayed? What if something awful had happened? When the message light came on she accessed the voice mail. JD's voice came on the line.

"Hi, Monica. JD. I have some business that I have to take care—" Then the line went dead.

Monica listened again, just in case she could hear the rest of the message, but it cut off in the same place. He had business. Did that mean he wasn't coming?

She wrapped up the dinner and put it away then went to her studio to take her mind off things, but it didn't work so she decided to watch TV. She was flipping channels when Baxter started barking. She scolded him to stop, but he refused and soon she heard the same noise that had agitated him. She put the TV on mute as the sound grew closer. Then through the window she saw a beam of light cascading over the ground. She opened the front door and saw a helicopter landing in the distance. *It couldn't be.* Her heart leaped when she saw the silhouette of a man exit and wave to the person inside then head toward the house.

Monica raced into the bathroom and checked her reflection to make sure everything was in place. She adjusted her head wrap then she bounded down the porch stairs and threw herself into his arms. "You came."

JD laughed, evidently pleased by her response. "I told you I would." She reached for one of his bags, but he moved it out of reach. Baxter jumped around him.

JD bent down to greet him. "Good to see you, buddy!" He lifted him up then stopped. "Wait a minute." He set the dog down and looked up at her, surprised. "What's he doing here?"

"He lives here now. I think you should adopt him."

He stood. "You do?"

She nodded. "He ran away from the shelter, and I knew he would keep doing that because he considers this place home. So I thought he could stay here until you made things official."

"I see." He rested his arm around her shoulders. "We'll talk about that later. I'm glad to be here."

"You're late," she said as they walked into the foyer.

He sighed, and for the first time she saw how tired he looked. "I know. I'm sorry." He dropped his bags and drew her close. "Forgive me?"

"Only this time."

He buried his face in her neck. "Mmm...good. You're nice and warm."

"But what kept you—"

He placed a finger over her lips. "Shh, no questions, remember?"

She kissed his finger. "I remember." Monica slipped out of his grasp and headed for the kitchen. "Let me go heat up some food."

JD unbuttoned his shirt. "Do you really think I came all this way just to eat?"

Monica stared at him and saw a devilish gleam in his eyes. She backed away as he approached her, unable to stop a smile. "But I cooked so much food."

He tossed his shirt aside, his smoldering eyes never leaving her face. "I'll eat it later."

"Sweet potato casserole and roasted turkey."

His heated gaze scaled the length of her as if she was a hundred-dollar bill and he was a broke man. "It can wait."

"You mean you're not even a little bit hungry?"

"Baby, I'm ravenous." He lunged for her.

She escaped him with a shriek. "You'll need your strength."

"I'm strong enough." He grabbed her and covered her mouth, his hand slipping down her dress.

She pulled away, remembering the bright kitchen lights. "We can't do this here."

He unzipped her dress. "It's working for me so far."

"Let's go upstairs."

"I have condoms with me."

"I have something else for you upstairs."

"I don't need anything else right now. All I want is you."

She pinched him. "You can have me upstairs."

JD let out a fierce growl. "All right. Let's go. Fast." He lifted her up in his arms. "Which room?"

"You don't need to carry me."

"Either I carry you or take you right here."

"Okay, okay," she said quickly when he started to set her down.

"Which room?"

"Yours." Earlier she'd made sure to close the drapes.

He took her up the stairs and set her on the bed. "Satisfied?"

"For now." She closed the door, removed her dress then stood in front of him. "The rest is up to you."

JD took that as his cue and spent the next two hours

satisfying her in ways she didn't know possible. The touch of his hand, the feel of his mouth, the way his body covered hers filled her with pure, explosive pleasure.

"You like that?" he said when she moaned.

"Oh, yes."

"Tell me what you're thankful for," he whispered.

"I can hardly think."

"I'll tell you what I'm thankful for. I'm thankful that you like when I do this." His hand roved down the back of her thighs. "And this." His hand slid between her legs. "And especially when I do this." He let two fingers slip inside. "I'll be even more thankful," he said in a hoarse whisper, "the day I get to see your face when you come."

Monica closed her eyes, unable to speak, her body trembling from the wondrous sensation. She drew him close and kissed him then whispered against his lips. "Please don't regret this moment."

"I won't regret a thing. I just wish—"

Monica didn't want him to be disappointed about anything, so she said, "Your wish is my command, master."

He laughed. "So you're a genie now?"

"Yes. I'm all yours. Close your eyes and see me with your hands." She grabbed his hands and placed them on her face. "Do I not please you, master?"

"You please me very much."

"I want to please you even more." She kissed him, wanting him to forget that they could make love only in the dark, that she had secrets to hide and that this time wouldn't last. She touched him in places so that he'd remember her when she wasn't with him. She wanted to claim every part of his body as hers.

Once finished, JD lay on his back, spellbound. "My Cinderella girl," he said then drifted off to sleep.

The next day they ate Monica's Thanksgiving meal and JD treated her to a vanilla-custard strawberry shortcake, made with fresh biscuits, and a berry-flecked pudding with angel food cake he'd had specially ordered from Wisconsin. The next three days were spent eating and finding inventive places throughout the house to make love—the darkened basement, an alcove in the attic, the walk-in closet in the master bedroom.

"I want you to do something for me," JD said as he packed his bag.

"What?"

"I have a friend's birthday coming up and I'd like to give her a necklace."

"Do you think I'll let you give another woman jewelry?"

"She's an old friend and I'd like to give her one of your designs." When she hesitated, he said, "I'll pay you for it."

"I don't need money."

"I'll pay you anyway."

"What does she like?"

"Anything sparkling."

"Okay, I'll do it."

He kissed her. "Thank you. See you at Christmas."

Christmas seemed like forever. There were only four weeks between Thanksgiving and Christmas, but Monica missed him. She missed his touch, his caresses, his smile. Everything about him. Fortunately, her assignment kept her busy. She wanted to make JD's friend a gorgeous necklace and make JD proud. And when Christmas came and Monica showed him the necklace, he was speechless.

"I don't know what to say."

She hugged him. "Good."

He took out his checkbook and wrote out an amount. Monica saw it and shook her head. "That's too much. I told you I don't need your money."

"This is business. Take the money."

She took it. "I'll frame it then."

He snatched it back. "No, if you're just going to put it on a wall, I'll invest it for you."

And they let the conversation drop, not wanting to spoil their limited time together.

JD was amazed with the transformation of the house. Monica had spent a lot of time and money decorating every room with Christmas decorations. He especially liked the pair of "holiday" briefs she had placed at the edge of his bed wrapped with a large red bow. Beginning with the large wreath hanging on the front door, to the red-and-green-striped shower curtain, bathroom mat and towels Monica brought back memories of the wonderful Christmases he had spent with his grandparents during the holidays.

That morning they sat in front of a roaring fire, the scent of a cinnamon broom Monica had purchased filling the air, and exchanged gifts. Monica's gift to him was a coupon for a massage.

"I wasn't sure what to get you," she said.

He flipped the coupon over. "Where do I have to go to redeem this?"

She grinned. "You don't have to go anywhere."

He lifted a sly brow. "Am I looking at my masseuse?"

She rubbed her hands together. "I'll take good care of you."

"You always do," he said, and then he followed her to the attic alcove, their favorite spot to make love.

It took them several hours before they returned to the family room, where JD gave Monica her gift. He sat on the couch wearing just a towel while Monica wore a full white terry robe. She opened the box JD handed her. Her heart fell when she saw the object. "A cell phone?"

He nodded. "So that I can reach you any time and you can call me. I have my private numbers programmed in. I don't like you alone at the farmhouse with only that landline to depend on. And you'll like this. I gave it a special ringtone. Listen."

JD dialed and soon the sound of the catbird filled the air. Monica laughed, realizing how wonderful his gift was. It was unique and it had been made just for her. She'd been used to expensive clothes, designer chocolates, pearls, large bouquets of flowers, but this moment would always stay with her. She hugged him. "Thank you."

"I also have another project for you. I have a friend who wants a special jewelry set her for her wedding. Do you think you could get something together in three weeks?"

Monica feigned a frown. "Should I worry about all these female friends of yours?"

JD nuzzled her neck. "Not a chance. No one compares to you." And the next several days he made sure she believed him.

Since Monica refused to travel, JD brought the world to her doorstep. On New Year's Eve, JD surprised her by having a selection of famous Southern dishes prepared by a world famous chef and delivered that day. Early in the morning he surprised her with a gift.

"Open it."

"JD, what is it?"

"You'll find out."

Monica gingerly tore open the wrapping paper to reveal an exquisitely embroidered summer dress. She knew it had cost him a fortune.

She held it against her. "It's beautiful, but I have nowhere to wear it to."

"Yes, you do. You're going to wear it tonight. Be ready by 6:00 p.m. sharp. I'll pick you up then."

"JD, you know I don't want to go out…"

"I know. Trust me. I have it all planned."

That evening, JD drove up in his small sports car. Monica wore the lime-green cashmere coat he'd bought her, hiding the new dress underneath. He drove her to the back of their property, where a small white tent had been erected.

When JD raised the door flap to the entrance, Monica stood speechless. Inside was an elegant dining setting: a glass table, two chairs, white silk tablecloth and napkins, and fine chinaware. Off to the side stood a row of heating containers where the food was being kept warm. Propane lanterns lit the intimate setting while soft music played in the background.

"When did you do all this?"

"I have my ways." He held out his hand. "Madam, are you ready to begin?"

"Certainly."

"May I remove your coat?"

She did, and it was JD's turn to be speechless. "Just like Cinderella."

She sat down. "And you're my prince?"

"I'm trying to be."

"You already are."

JD played the role of the waiter, and later that evening her lover. It was a night to remember. Neither knew when the New Year arrived, and neither cared.

On Valentine's Day JD gave her a trunk full of the most elegant bedroom boudoir sets Monica had ever seen. She wore a different one for the three nights he was there. Monica began to believe that a love this strong couldn't be broken and that she had nothing left to fear. But she was wrong.

"You don't look happy to see us," Crystalline said when JD opened the door to his apartment.

"I'm just busy."

She kissed him on the cheek and stepped inside. "You have three bigger places than this. Why do you stay here?"

"Because I like it." He knew his mother thought the place was too small because she liked a lot of space, but she'd have thought the Titanic was just "cozy."

"Yes, and you're always busy."

"But this time more busy than usual," Donnie said, following behind his mother.

JD scowled. "What's that supposed to mean?"

"It's just an observation," Crystalline said to ease the tension between the two men. "No reason to get upset."

"I'm not upset." JD closed the door and watched them take a seat.

"We just haven't seen you. It's almost summer and every time I try to reach you, you're out of town."

"What have you been doing?" Donnie said bluntly.

JD sat on the couch that faced them. "Working."

Donnie picked up a book resting on the coffee table. "Not just work." He held up a book about eye disease and shook his head in disgust. "Don't tell me you're still seeing that dumpy, I mean Dulane lady," he hastily corrected when his brother shot him a look. "I know that after that she-devil Stacy anything would look good, but—"

"We just want you to be happy," Crystalline said.

"I am." He laughed, surprised by the admission. "Yes, I'm actually happy." *Dad, I finally did it! I'm happy.* Just thinking about Monica put a smile on his face. He found himself thinking about her at the strangest times. Once he'd found himself in his office remembering the feel of Monica's soft skin, her smell, the softness of her fingers as they roamed the length of his body, when he was supposed to be closing a major investment deal.

Her succulent kisses could make him hard for days. Even in the darkness, he knew she was a thing of beauty, and he wondered why she kept her exquisite body hidden. He wanted to draw her out, but he knew that would take time. One day he'd see all of her.

"I hope she knows how lucky she is," his mother said.

"I'm the lucky one."

His mother forced a grin, but the expression in her eyes showed worry.

Donnie noticed that look as he and his mother left JD's apartment. A light April rain fell outside.

"You're really worried about him, aren't you?" he said.

"He's a grown man, I know. It's just something about *her*."

Donnie nodded, but he didn't know what to say. He couldn't understand why a plain woman like Monica would concern his mother and have his brother fall head over heels. But something was definitely up. It was rare that his mother invited him to have a "family chat" with JD. Usually it was the other way around, with JD and his mother coming to his place to try to set him straight on an issue. But he loved his brother and didn't want to see him made a fool of. He'd find out what that Dulane woman was all about.

Chapter 12

Gerald suppressed a yawn. The woman didn't stop talking. He looked around the house of Lavinia Walker, an attractive socialite in her mid-fifties who'd moved in Venus's circles. She was easy to flirt with and desperate for attention. The more he complimented her, the more information she gave him. Unfortunately, it wasn't the information he wanted. He set down his coffee cup and feigned interest as she rattled on about her husband's travels. He glanced around the sitting room, and his gaze fell on a newspaper lying on the side table. He picked it up to hide another yawn.

He blinked his eyes and was about to put it down, but he stopped when he saw a pretty woman in a wedding dress wearing an extraordinary necklace. He recognized the design and pattern. No other woman had that distinct style. After researching Venus's life for over a year, he could recognize her work from the sketches she'd done while married to Delong; she utilized the unmistakable style of her great-great-grandmother. "Who is this?"

Lavinia looked at the picture he held up. "Oh, my niece. She just had a fabulous wedding in Portugal. You should have seen—"

"That's an amazing necklace she's wearing," Gerald said before she could change the topic.

"Yes, a gift from a dear friend of ours."

Gerald felt his palms tingle with anticipation. Could this be it? Could he finally have found a trail that wasn't a dead end? Had Venus sent this anonymously? "Then you're very fortunate. I know my girlfriend would love something like it."

"Exquisite, isn't it? It's one of a kind and—"

"Yes," he said quickly, wishing she'd stop referring to the damn necklace and give him a name. "Who gave it to her again?"

"It's from a brilliant new designer who is slowly emerging. I don't know her name."

"She sent it to your niece anonymously?" he asked, trying to get the story straight.

"Oh, no," Lavinia said with a laugh. "I told you it was from a friend of ours."

Gerald took a deep breath. "Which friend?"

"JD Rozan, of course," she said as though he should have been able to guess. "He's been talking about her for months. He's very proud of his new discovery."

Gerald grinned, wanting to kiss her. The chatterbox had given him a new lead. "I bet he is."

Monica heard a car drive up just as she finished drying Baxter after his bath. It wasn't a holiday. She'd just seen JD on Memorial Day, when they'd spent time together remembering those they knew who had served in the military and those who still served. So she knew it wasn't JD and she wasn't expecting anyone else. She glanced out the window and saw a silver car she didn't recognize. *Breathe,* she told herself. *I'm sure it's nothing.* She took off her apron and glanced down at Baxter. She pointed to the front door. "Attack!"

Baxter wagged his tail.

Monica rested her hands on her hips. "You have absolutely no guard-dog instincts."

The doorbell rang.

Monica took another deep breath and answered.

Donnie flashed a wide grin and took off his sunglasses. Behind him the hot June sun blazed bright. He radiated good looks and charm, accentuating his devil-may-care attitude with a leather jacket and jeans. "Hello, Monica. I was just in the neighborhood and I thought I'd stop by and say hello."

They both knew it was a lame line, but Monica didn't argue with him. "JD's not here."

"That's what I'm counting on." He glanced down at Baxter. "Is he friendly?"

"Sometimes."

Donnie bent down and petted him. To her annoyance, Baxter rolled over on his back for a belly rub. Donnie laughed and obliged him. "He's a lamb." He looked up at her. "So are you going to let me in or do I have to ask?"

He was family. He had more right to the place than she did. Monica opened the door wider and Donnie sauntered in with his thumbs hooked in his belt loops. "You've really added a nice touch to this place."

"What do you want?" she said in a flat tone.

He looked at her, offended. "Why would I want anything?"

Monica rested her hip against the door and waited, not willing to play his game. "What do you want?" she repeated, this time slowly.

"A drink would be nice."

She closed the door. He was as infuriating as his brother. She released a fierce sigh and said, "I don't have any liquor."

"Yes, you do. You just don't know where to look." He went into the family room and walked over to the bookshelf. He hit a side panel and a bottom door swung open. He pulled out a glass and a bottle of brandy. "Want some?"

"No, thanks," she said, trying to hide her surprise. She hadn't even known Nadine liked to drink.

"This is my grandpa's secret," Donnie said as if he'd read her mind. "I saw him do it once and coerced him to tell me the trick. I helped him stock it."

"And empty it, no doubt."

Donnie shrugged, unfazed by her disapproval. "Wouldn't want it to go to waste." He poured himself a drink then sat down. "Yes, you've made it real cozy here."

Monica folded her arms. "Do I really have to ask you a third time?"

He grinned. "I heard that's the charm."

"What do you want, Donnie?"

Donnie took a long swallow then set his glass aside.

"Okay, since you're not one for small talk, I'll tell you why I'm here."

She took a seat. "I'm listening."

"You've put my brother under a spell, and I want to know how you did it. And what you're up to."

"I didn't do anything and I'm not up to anything."

He poured himself another drink. "See, I want to believe you," he said with a sigh of regret. "But the Rozan brothers aren't really lucky when it comes to women. We can get them, we just can't trust them. I can tell my mother doesn't trust you. My brother trusts you with his life." He set his glass down and leaned forward. "I'm here to find out who to believe."

"I don't have to prove anything to you."

His charming features turned hard, and the look in his eyes sent a chill through her. "That's where you're wrong. I love my brother. He's a good man and I've seen women use him. I'm not saying he's gullible or anything. He knows what they're about and doesn't care. I mean with Stacy he learned early that she was using him because she hoped that she could persuade him to use his money and influence to protect her father. She found out she was wrong. He doesn't let his heart get involved. But this time—with you—it's a different story. I won't let him get hurt. He's got money, power, prestige. Which one are you after?"

"I'm not after anything." She stood. "Are we through here?"

Donnie rested back and crossed his legs at the ankles. He glanced around. "What do you two do around here? Watch the grass grow? Count pebbles?"

Monica bristled, defensive. "We go for bicycle rides,

long walks, watch the sunset, eat good food. Enjoy each other's company."

"That's it?"

"That's all I'm going to tell you." She headed for the door.

"He's worried about your eyes, you know." He nodded when she turned to him in surprise. "He's got a bunch of books on eye care, and I won't be surprised if he's also gone online and spoken to specialists."

Monica sighed, both exasperated and pleased by how much JD cared. "He doesn't need to worry about me. I get along fine. Always have."

Donnie sat up and sniffed the air. "Mmm...something smells good."

Monica checked her watch. "I almost forgot my zucchini bread." She ran into the kitchen and pulled it out. She set her oven mittens aside and checked to make sure it was done.

Donnie stood in the kitchen doorway. "You know, I'm really good at sampling."

"It has to cool first."

He rested his arms on the kitchen island as if he had all the time in the world. "I can wait."

"I don't feed men who don't trust me."

"How about men who trust you a little?"

"I can give them a crumb."

Donnie laughed. "I can see why my brother likes you. Okay, I believe you, but it'll take more to convince my mother."

"She doesn't have to worry about JD and me. It's nothing serious. No one was even supposed to know about it."

"JD didn't say anything, it's just that we knew something was up and made a guess." He looked at the bread. "Is it ready now?

"Give it another two minutes. Try to keep yourself busy."

"Doing what?"

Monica glanced down at the dog by his side. "Play with Baxter."

Donnie got down on all fours and played with Baxter, who jumped around him and tugged on his favorite toy. "He's great." He stood and picked him up. That's when Baxter peed on him.

"I change my mind."

Monica saw Donnie's face and burst into laughter.

"You think this is funny?"

Monica laughed harder as the stain continued to spread on the front of his jeans.

He set Baxter on the floor. "You trained him to do that, didn't you?"

"No. You got him overexcited. Come on, I'll get you another pair to wear and put those in the wash."

"Just get me a towel. JD's clothes never fit me. And I'm not leaving until I get a slice of that zucchini bread."

"I'll give you two."

JD first noticed the car then he heard the laughter. He'd wanted to surprise Monica, but it seemed he was the one in for the surprise. He opened the front door and was greeted by a deep masculine laugh mixed with a lighter feminine one. He'd never made Monica laugh like that, and a cool, possessive anger slowly swept through him. He briefly petted Baxter, who had come up to greet him, then set his bag down. Monica and her companion were so engrossed in each other they didn't even hear him enter. He turned the corner and saw Monica and Donnie on the couch gripped in peals of laughter. The scene tore at him. He'd never seen such pure delight on her face. He'd never been able to make her laugh like that.

This place had been their private sanctum where he'd made her smile, but Donnie had taken his place.

Donnie saw him first and shot to his feet. "JD."

"What are you doing here?" Monica said, also rising.

"Thought I'd surprise you," he said in a low voice, his gaze dipping to the towel wrapped around his brother's waist.

Donnie noticed the look and shook his head. "It's not what you think."

JD folded his arms and nodded. "Excuse me." He turned and walked out the front door. He had to get away from them. He had to get away from the scene that would now burn in his memory. He'd never felt jealous before, but the monster was slowly consuming him. All he saw was Monica's forehead on Donnie's shoulder, her hand on his leg. He wouldn't be angry at Monica. It wasn't her fault she'd fallen for Donnie's charms.

"JD, slow down."

He turned and saw Donnie running after him as he struggled to keep his towel in place. JD stopped and pointed at him. "Why did you come here?"

"I just wanted to check her out."

"Why?"

"Because Mom thinks she's hiding something."

"I *know* she's hiding something. I don't care. I have a few secrets myself."

"No, you don't. I bet that woman knows everything about you. You're making yourself too vulnerable."

"When did I ask for your advice?"

"I'm giving it to you anyway. I like her, too." He held up a hand. "Just as a friend. Nothing happened. I—"

JD grabbed Donnie by the front of his shirt and shoved him against his car. "Stay away from her."

Donnie searched his brother's face, clearly bewildered. "What is wrong with you? You know I'd never move in on one of your women."

JD released him. "You may not mean to, but you have."

"When? How?"

JD turned away, feeling like a fool. "It doesn't matter."

"Come on, man," Donnie pressed. "Talk to me. What did I do?"

"I've never made her laugh like that. You, Dad, Gran can make a room light up. You get people to like you without effort. That's not easy for me, and you just showed me how far I am from making her truly happy."

Donnie sighed and shook his head. "Brother, you think too much. I may make her laugh, but she loves you."

JD's gaze sharpened. "Did she say that?"

"She doesn't have to. We spent most of the time talking about you. I mean, she made this delicious zucchini bread—"

"She baked for you?"

"It was a new recipe she was trying out for your next visit. I see why you like her."

JD snatched the towel away. What he saw made him grip it in his fist. "What happened?" he said in a low voice.

Donnie covered his exposed front, his face turning red. "My underpants got wet, too."

"Really?"

"Your dog peed on me and everything got stained. She offered to wash them."

JD nodded. "I see."

"Come on," Donnie begged, glancing around. "Don't be like that."

"Don't ever come back here without telling me."

"I won't."

"I don't believe you." JD headed toward the front door.

"I won't! I won't! I promise."

JD tossed him the towel over his shoulder with a triumphant grin. "Good."

Monica met him at the front door. "Your brother's things are ready now."

"He's coming," JD said, jerking his head toward his brother, who was fighting the wind from blowing his towel up.

Monica giggled at the sight. JD sent her a pensive look. "You like him?"

"Very much."

JD nodded then walked past her. Moments later Donnie ran up the porch stairs. Monica handed him his jeans and underwear. "Thanks," he said with a rueful grin.

She covered her mouth to keep from laughing again. "You're welcome."

"I'll be back in a minute," he said and darted down the hall.

Chapter 13

Monica went into the kitchen and found JD considering the zucchini bread.

"Do you want me to cut you a slice?"

He didn't look up. "Maybe later."

She walked up to him and wrapped her arms around his waist, resting her cheek against his back. "So what's the special occasion? Is there a holiday I've forgotten about?"

He turned to her, his voice low and his gaze steady. "No. I just wanted to see you."

Monica loosened a button on her blouse. "And how much of me do you want to see?"

"As much as I can." He slid his hand up her blouse and unlatched her bra.

She pulled away. "Careful, your brother is still here."

He drew her close. "I'll tell him to leave."

"You can't."

He paused. "Why not?"

"He's staying for lunch."

"What?"

"I asked him to stay for lunch."

"You mean if I hadn't come you would have had lunch with him?"

Monica raised her voice in mock horror. "Yes, imagine the scandal."

JD turned to the counter. "I think I'll take a slice of that bread."

Donnie came into the kitchen. "Well, I'd better go."

JD opened a drawer and grabbed a knife. "Yes, see you later."

"You'll go after lunch," Monica corrected, gathering the dishes.

Donnie cast JD a nervous look. "I don't—"

"I insist." She handed him the plates and utensils. "Go set up the table."

He hesitated then left.

JD watched him go then glared at her. "Why are you doing this?"

"To show you there's no reason to be jealous."

He gripped the knife in his hands. "What makes you think I'm jealous?"

Monica gently took the knife from him. "I have no idea," she said with a note of sarcasm. She placed the knife back in the drawer. "You can have the bread after lunch."

"But I want it now." He opened the drawer.

She slammed it shut. "You'll have to wait."

They faced each other in a battle of wills. "Don't push me, Monica."

She cupped his face in her hand and made her voice firm. "And don't insult me, JD."

"I'm not—"

"This is how it's going to work. You're going to eat lunch with your brother and me like a grown man, and you'll be civil or else."

He began to grin, amused by her threat. "Or else what?"

"You can go home right now."

His grin disappeared. "This isn't supposed to be about anyone but us."

"I know, and it will be once I get your brother to fully trust me. I can't afford to have him or your mother asking questions about me."

"If you were in danger, would you let me know?"

Monica thought for a moment then nodded. "If I thought you could help me, yes."

"I can do a lot of things. In case you've forgotten, I'm a rich and powerful man with a few enemies. I don't mind having one more."

But Monica knew Anton wasn't a normal adversary. JD dealt in the world of business. There was corruption and greed, revenge and betrayal. But she was certain he'd never had to deal with a killer before. She didn't want him to think about what she was hiding from him, so she lightly kissed him on the mouth and whispered against his lips. "Are you staying for lunch?"

He raised his brows, and she could tell he wanted to resume their conversation, but he let his shoulders fall. "Fine. I'll stay. But I want my zucchini bread. Now."

She took out the knife, cut him a large slice and slipped it on a plate. "There."

"Thank you."

Monica picked up a container of potato salad from out of the fridge. "Now let's eat."

Lunch started out as a disaster. JD refused to talk, and every topic Monica tried with Donnie fell flat. After nearly a half hour, Monica kicked JD under the table, eager to get his cooperation. He ignored her, so she kicked him again—harder. He set his fork down and rested his arms on the table. "Hey, Donnie, ever heard about the guy from Manassas?"

Donnie looked at him, curious. "No."

"Well, there once was a guy from Manassas," he said then commenced to tell him a limerick so dirty that both Donnie and Monica were left speechless then Donnie burst into laughter. Monica soon followed suit.

"You sick bastard," Donnie said in good humor.

JD held up his hands. "I didn't make it up."

"Tell me another one."

He told them five more until they had tears running down their faces. They finished lunch in the dining room and ended up in the family room, where Donnie showed JD where their grandfather had hidden the liquor and JD showed Donnie where he'd kept his stash of cigars. Monica and Baxter watched as the two brothers reminisced about their past.

"Remember when Dad taught us how to fish?" Donnie asked.

JD nodded. "And you were upset because you hadn't caught anything, so Dad gave you his fish and let Mom and Gran think that you'd caught it."

"Mom made me a big ice-cream sundae. I didn't stop grinning for days."

"Dad always did stuff like that. Remember how he used to leave us letters under the door that he wrote as Santa Claus?"

Donnie sat up. "They *were* from Santa Claus. I don't know what you got, but mine were real."

JD shook his head with a smile. "So gullible. No wonder you get into trouble, little brother."

Donnie laughed then held up his hand. "Wait. There was a song he liked to play." He bit his lip and furrowed his brow trying to recall it. "I can't remember its name."

"I think I know the one." JD took out the guitar left in the closet and began to play a classic Southern lullaby.

Donnie let out a long sigh. "Yes, that's it. I hadn't heard that in years."

JD started to put the guitar back in its case then stopped. He took a deep breath then walked over to the guitar stand and rested it there. They sat in silence, letting the good memories of their father and Gran fill the quiet.

Donnie stood. "It's time I headed home." He walked to the front door then turned to his brother. "Don't be a stranger."

"Right."

"You can't leave empty-handed," Monica said and disappeared into the kitchen. She came back with several slices of zucchini bread wrapped in foil.

"Thank you," he said then hugged her.

"It's just bread."

"That's not for the bread."

"What's it for?"

"It's for giving me something back I didn't even

know I'd lost," he said. Then he quickly kissed her on the mouth. "That's for the bread."

JD took a step forward and rested a possessive hand on Monica's shoulder. "Do that again and I will kill you."

Donnie grinned then jogged to his car. Within minutes he was gone. JD and Monica spent the rest of their unexpected holiday in bed, and they did the same after seeing the fireworks on the Fourth of July.

Before he arrived, Monica wanted to make it her own independence day as well. She wasn't the same Monica she'd once been. She'd been careful in how she improved her appearance over the past several months, still not wanting to reveal who she was, but she had emerged a different woman.

Although JD hadn't said anything, he had bought her silk scarves, brilliantly colored cashmere sweaters, flowing Indian-made skirts and African batik dresses to add color to her wardrobe. At times she wanted to shed her disguise and show him who she really was, but she did not give in to the temptation. She had to preserve her image. It was too dangerous otherwise. But tonight she had dressed in a loose peach dress and made one concession that symbolized freedom. She took off her head wrap and let her hair fall free. Not in its signature Venus style—pressed bone straight—but in its natural state with its slight wave pattern that made it look a little wild.

When JD came through the door and saw her, he stopped. "I'm sorry, Miss. I thought a Ms. Dulane lived here." He took a step back to leave. "I obviously have the wrong address."

Monica laughed and grabbed his hand. She pulled him inside. "Do you like it?"

He lifted her hair up and let her midnight tresses cascade through his fingers. "You should never wrap your hair ever again. You're beautiful."

Not *it's* beautiful. But *you're* beautiful. She wondered if he was aware of the slip, but she didn't care. She was happy to please him. At least this part of her life was real.

"Why have you kept it up so long?"

"Time. It takes a lot of care, and I'm usually too busy to bother. So I just braid it up and put on a wrap."

"Tonight I'm going to show you off." JD took Monica to a small, cozy restaurant about ten minutes out of town and then to a private location to see the fireworks. It was a warm summer evening, and when they returned home they made fireworks of their own.

JD held Monica close and looked up into the darkness. "Do you want to know what JD stands for?"

She nodded. "I've always been curious."

"Want to guess?"

"I'd need a hint first."

"I was named after a stone."

Monica thought for a moment then cringed. "Oh, no. Not Jasper."

He nodded. "Yes, my mother named me after a stone and my father named me after a fir tree."

"The Douglas fir?"

He nodded again. "My full name is Jasper Douglas Rozan." He held up a finger. "And you're *never* allowed to call me that."

Monica laughed. "Not even in the heat of passion?"

"Especially not then."

"I'll try to remember."

"You'd better. I'll never rise again if you do."

She slipped her hand down his thigh. "I think I'd manage to persuade you."

He covered her hand. "Maybe, but I won't be happy about it."

Monica fell quiet a moment then licked her lips, unsure of her next question. "Why did you tell me?"

"I just thought my wife should know."

Monica stiffened. "Your wife?"

He stroked her back in a lazy, sensual motion. "You don't like the idea?"

Monica shook her head. "It's not that. It's just…there are so many things we don't know about each other."

"You know more about me than I know about you?"

"Is that a challenge?"

"No, just an observation."

"If you want this to last, the less you know about me the better."

"You know we can't keep this up forever."

"I didn't expect it to last forever."

"I see."

"JD, marriage is a big step, and I can't be part of your world—"

"You wouldn't have to be part of it. I wouldn't expect you to host parties or go to major events with me. I have other places I want to show you. You could live wherever you want and you'd always be safe with me. I can protect you."

But who would protect him?

"I know it's a lot to think about," JD said when she didn't reply. "So I'll let you get used to the idea."

Monica wasn't sure she would. He wanted to marry her? Did that mean he loved her? And would he still love her when she revealed the truth that she wasn't really a scared, dowdy jeweler, but an international symbol of beauty? Would he love Venus, whose fame would eclipse his own? If she told him the truth about why she was hiding, would he think that she was using him? Would he think that had been her agenda all along? His brother had said that he was used to women with hidden agendas. Maybe he'd be jaded enough to think she was one of them.

Even if she dared to hope that he would accept her without her disguise, she knew she would be putting his life in danger. She knew the lengths Anton would go to get what he wanted, and that he'd stop at nothing. Tears filled her eyes. She'd found a man whom she desperately loved but couldn't have. But tonight she wanted to dream. She wanted to believe that anything was possible.

"Yes, I will marry you."

JD sat up. "What? Really?"

"Yes. I can't marry you now, but know that I want to."

"We can—"

Monica pressed her fingers against his lips. "Don't make any plans. No one else can know. Just you. This is a secret you cannot share."

"So that means no engagement ring?"

"No."

"How about three dozen roses?"

"No."

"An orchestra?"

Monica laughed and held him tight. "No. I don't need any of those things. You're enough for me."

JD gathered her close, and she relaxed into the cushion of his embrace. "And I'm yours forever."

His words echoed in her heart and mind, and she tried to fight back the pain of loss, knowing that she would soon have to leave him.

Chapter 14

Venus was here. He'd traced her to the little touristy town in Georgia. It was a far cry from the lavish lifestyle she'd led. He could make a call to Stevens and let him know about his success, but part of him was reluctant to let the chase end. He hadn't seen sight of her yet, but he knew she was staying at the Rozan farmhouse. He picked up his mobile phone then set it down. There was plenty of time to talk to Stevens. Venus wasn't going anywhere, and one more day wouldn't matter.

What he needed now was a drink. His part of the job was over. He'd been hired to locate her—that's all. It was Stevens's job to figure out how to take her down. Gerald walked into the local bar, which was crowded with tourists and some locals. He ordered a drink then settled into a position where he could watch the other patrons and the main street. He wanted to find out more about Venus. What did the locals think of her? Did she have any friends? Who were the people she trusted? Perhaps someone here could fill in some of those details for him.

He looked around to consider his options. It was easy to separate the tourists from the locals—the tourists looked happy. He spotted one fat guy on his third beer sitting with two younger men. One guy looked half-asleep while the other guy with a knife tattoo looked as if he could go many more rounds. No, he wasn't a candidate. He couldn't picture Venus talking to him. Gerald shifted his gaze and saw another guy. He was thin and looked as if the world was about to collapse on him. He could sense his desperation from across the room. A fresh-faced woman sat beside him. He knew the type. The strong, I'll-stay-by-your-side type of woman whom men could depend on. She turned and spoke to the man in a low voice, and both of them kept glancing at the general store across the street.

Was there trouble there? He had to find out because people in trouble always wanted a solution, and that would be his trump card to get the information he wanted. Gerald strolled over to their table and held out his hand. "Hi, folks, I'm Michael Dodds and I'm here to invest in small businesses around town. Could you tell me who owns that store across the street?" He saw the man's face come to light and knew he'd hit on the right angle.

"I do," the man said. "I'm William Hostie and this is my wife, Treena Ikes."

"Mind if I join you?"

William eagerly grabbed another chair and gestured to it. "Please sit down."

"So you're thinking of investing, huh?"

"Yes."

Treena watched him as she took a sip of her drink. "What made you decide on here? Not many people are interested."

"Wherever there are tourists, I hear the sound of money."

"Me, too. I have lots of plans for my store that I could tell you about."

"I'd be happy to hear them. I've had a chance to look around. The town has a pretty impressive craft fair."

"Comes every summer. We have lots of craftsmen around here."

"I heard that JD Rozan has property close by. Is he looking to invest, too?"

He saw Treena's eyes narrow with suspicion and knew he had to tread more carefully, but her husband's face changed, reflecting a completely different emotion—hate. "He doesn't care about this place."

"That's not what I heard."

"He likes to pretend that this town matters to him because of his grandparents' land. But he's not attached to it like the rest of us."

"That's funny. I thought he was helping a local woman get established here."

Treena leaned forward. "Why are you so interested in what JD's doing? That's no concern of yours."

Gerald smiled. "I don't want to step on anyone's toes. JD's got some big contacts along the East Coast, and let's just say I wouldn't want to get in his way. I like to know how things are run before I jump."

"You don't have to worry about JD," William said.

"And yes, there's a woman at the Rozan place, but she's not one of us."

"Why not?"

"She keeps to herself. Sort of strange. Isn't that right, Treena?"

Treena took another sip of her drink and remained silent.

Gerald knew he'd lost her support. Fortunately, he still had her husband, and instinctively he knew he could get whatever he wanted from him, as long as he swung the promise of money in front of him. Gerald pretended to look at his watch. "I have to go, but this has been nice. I'd like to talk to you some more about your business." He handed William his card, but his wife took it instead. She didn't trust him, but that was fine. Venus had run out of time.

Monica hesitated when she first heard the knock on her door. She didn't receive visitors. She looked through the peephole and saw Treena. She opened the door. "I didn't know vets made house calls for small pets," she said in a light voice.

Treena didn't smile. "I didn't come about Baxter. I have to talk to you."

Monica stepped back and allowed her to enter. "Sure."

Treena glanced behind her then stepped in and closed the door. "This is probably none of my business, but I don't trust him even though William does. You may not be one of us, but you mean more to this community than any stranger does."

Monica frowned. "What are you talking about?"

"I'm sorry. I know I'm babbling, but I've just never been part of something like this before. I might be blowing it out of proportion."

Monica sighed, trying to be patient. "Blowing what out of proportion?"

"There's a man who at first was talking about JD, but I caught on that his real interest is you."

Monica froze. "What does he look like?"

"Medium height, brown-skinned." She frowned. "Unremarkable really. Nothing about him stood out."

Monica began to relax. That didn't sound like Anton, but obviously he'd put someone on her trail.

"What has he been saying?"

"Just asking about your business, and he's been seducing William with promises of investing in new or struggling businesses. We certainly need the money and at first it sounded all right, but there was something about him I didn't like. He tried to hint that he knew how JD did business and then started asking about you." She flexed her fingers. "I don't know why you're here, but I just thought you should know. If he's an ex-husband or something, I can call the cops."

Monica doubted Drent's cousin the sheriff would do anything to help her. "Thanks. I know what I need to do."

"Maybe you should call JD and—"

"No," Monica said quickly. "I can handle this on my own. Don't worry. I'll just need you to do one thing for me."

"What?" Treena said, frightened.

"Look after Baxter for me. Just for a couple weeks."

Treena's fear disappeared. "Okay. Are you sure you don't want to—"

"I'm sure. What did he say his name was?"

"Michael Dodds, and he's staying at Aunt Mabel's Bed and Breakfast. I found out from William's clerk Donna 'cause her mother owns the place."

"Thanks."

"What are you going to do?" she asked as she anxiously watched Monica gather Baxter's things.

"I'm not sure yet." Monica gave Treena a bag of Baxter's favorite toys then attached Baxter's leash to his collar and handed Treena the lead. "I really appreciate you doing this."

"I wish I could do more."

"You've done plenty." Monica gave her a quick hug. "I'll never forget it."

The moment Treena left, Monica began to pace. How had they found her here? She'd been so careful not to leave any clues. But that didn't matter now. She'd made an error somewhere. She had to change her plans and leave sooner than she'd anticipated. She left JD a note telling him how much she loved him and that she had to leave. Then she packed a few things. She had to turn the tables. She could no longer be the hunted. She had to become the huntress.

She had to get Anton's focus off this small town and the people she cared about. Monica had to disappear and let Venus emerge.

Gerald didn't dream much. He'd been too disappointed in the past to believe in dreams. But as he lay on his bed in the quaint bed and breakfast, he let his mind wander to what he would say when he spoke to Venus. He knew he wouldn't. He never let his targets see him. Otherwise, they would run again. But this target he wished he could talk to. She'd sent him on a merry chase he'd never forget.

"Michael Dodds?"

"Yeah?" he said in a lazy tone. The owner was probably calling him down for lunch or something. He turned toward the door then scrambled out of bed. Venus stood in the doorway. Tall, gorgeous, amazing. A grown man's wet dream dressed in a form-clinging leopard-print top and black skirt, ending in spiked high heels. Her catlike eyes studied him. If this cat claws, he didn't care about being mauled to death.

"Are you Michael Dodds?" she said again, her voice a low purr.

Gerald nodded, not trusting himself to speak. He didn't care how she'd found him or how she'd gotten the key to his room. He didn't want this moment to end.

"May I come in?"

Did she really have to ask? He absently gestured to a seat.

She walked into the room. Gerald's gaze dropped to the seductive sway of her hips and her long, sleek legs. She sat down. He licked his lips when her skirt inched up.

"Anton sent you to find me?"

"Yes," he managed in a hoarse voice. He cleared his throat and tucked his shirt in his trousers. "It hasn't been easy to find you."

She smiled. "I'm glad."

"Look, um…I hate to see it end this way, but—"

"You're just doing your job."

"Right."

"I want you to give him a message for me."

"What?"

"Tell him it ends in New York."

Chapter 15

Few things surprised Nikki Dupree. As an interior designer, she'd once worked for a professional, artsy couple who wanted to design everything around the color of their shih tzu and another client who didn't want anything with a square shape. But that evening when she opened her front door and saw her sister standing on the doorstep, she was gripped in shock.

"Nikki, I need to talk to you."

Nikki still didn't move. It had been nearly two years since she'd seen or heard from her sister. She had always regretted how she'd let Delong put a strain in their relationship. He'd wanted it that way. He liked to keep Monica for himself, but he was gone now and they had a second chance.

"Nikki?" Monica said, giving her a little shake.

Nikki shook her head and opened the door wider. "Sorry. Come in. I'm just so— Where have you been?"

"A lot of places, but I can't tell you about it right now. I need your help."

"My help?" Nikki said, once again stunned. Her sister rarely needed anything and especially not from her. Monica's life had been full of ease and privilege, but she'd never given her sister a reason to envy her. It was just how night followed day. Her sister was always generous and kind and gave to the family, but their lives were vastly different. Nikki had worked her way up to the position of international interior designer after starting out as a clerk in an exclusive furniture store several years earlier, but the challenge had been worth it.

She led Monica into the kitchen, noticing how uneasy she seemed. She quickly poured her some grape juice and led her to a seat. "I'm happy you came to see me."

Monica began to relax and took the glass from her. "I didn't mean to stay away."

Nikki sat down in front of her. "Then why did you?"

"It's a long story."

Nikki shrugged and tucked one leg under her, getting comfortable. "I've got all night."

Monica hesitated. "You may not believe me."

"I'll always believe you. Besides, this is a night of surprises. So go ahead and tell me."

Monica told her sister about her dinner with Anton, how she'd ended up on his compound and how she had escaped. She shared how she'd changed her identity and lived as Monica Dulane for over a year. She was careful not to mention anything about JD. Nikki stared at her, dumbfounded.

"You do believe me, don't you? I know it sounds crazy, but—"

"Of course I believe you. I just don't know what to say." She tapped the table. "I do know one thing. Anton needs to be taken out." She bit her lip. "I think I could find someone who would—"

Monica waved her hands. "No, I don't need you to find a hit man for me."

"It won't be any trouble and it won't cost that much."

"Nikki, that's too much of a risk."

"There are subtle ways to do it. I had a client whose ex-husband was making her life miserable. Her brother took care of it and he never bothered her again." She tapped her chin, pensive. "What was his name again?"

"I have my own plans for Anton."

"Plans? How can you have any plans? The guy is a lunatic. Anything you think you can do will be risky. Are you sure it was him who found you again?"

"Yes. He sent someone to Georgia to find me. I even met him."

Nikki's mouth fell open. "You talked to him?"

"Yes, I wanted him to know that I was on to them. I had to redirect their attention from the town to keep certain people who are important to me safe. That's why I'm here."

"What do you want me to do?"

"Anton's coming to New York because I sent him a message through the guy he had trail me that I'll be here. He won't be able to resist the challenge, but I can't meet him alone. I need to be seen so that people will start talking about Venus's return and draw him out. I need to know of any high-profile or high-society charity events or parties I can attend."

"There's a small, intimate gathering this weekend for the visiting Nigerian ambassador, the current recipient of the Nobel Peace Prize. He's being honored for his unfailing dedication to making the voice of the poor worldwide heard. I think he's some kind of literary genius."

Monica shook her head. "Too humanitarian. Anton wouldn't show up."

Nikki told her of five other events, and Monica chose two of them.

"Do you think you can get me in?"

"Have you forgotten that you're Venus? It won't be a problem. I know the organizers for both events and I'll have no problem getting you invited as a VIP. All I have to do is say Venus is in town. What else do you need?"

"I need you to come with me to my house. I have some clothes there and need to set up some things, but I don't want to be alone."

The house was just as she'd remembered. A looming, palatial mansion with numerous windows accented with gargoyles, like a gothic castle. It had been one of Delong's favorite locations when he was in the U.S. Monica passed by the front gate with ease, the guard staring at her as if she were a ghost. Her housekeeper fared no better. When Monica opened the front door, her housekeeper, Deidra LaSalle, screamed so loud that Monica feared the glass mirror in the hall would shatter.

"It's all right, Deidra, it's only me," Monica said while Nikki covered her ears.

"You're back!"

"Yes."

She gripped Monica in a fierce hug. Although Deidra was a small, stocky woman, she had the strength of two men.

"Deidra, I can't breathe," Monica said, imagining her ribs breaking from the smaller woman's exuberance.

Deidra released her and patted her face. She was a recent immigrant from Haiti and had been in the U.S. for only a short period, but she'd created a special bond with Monica the moment she met her.

"We didn't think you'd come back. But I know how much you loved your husband and you needed the time and space to grieve, so—"

"Yes," Monica interrupted, not wanting to talk about Delong. "I can't take time right now to explain. I just stopped by to get a few things."

"Everything is as you left it." Yes, she knew that Delong had everything set up so that things would run just as before after his death. She was well provided for.

"Thank you," Monica said as she headed to the stairs. "I'll let you know if I need anything."

"I'll let the chef know that you're here, and should I get Howard?"

He was the chauffer. "No, thank you, but dinner would be nice. Say around eight?"

"Yes, Mrs. Price," Deidra said then rushed away.

Nikki looked around at the arch stairway and extravagant drapery. "This must be an expensive place to keep up."

"I can afford it."

"You don't have to keep it as a monument to him."

Monica walked into her master bedroom. "I don't plan to."

"Then what will you do?" Nikki asked as she stepped into Monica's grand bedroom with its white plush carpeting and a sculpture of a goddess in the corner. "You'll have to change everything," Nikki said, looking around the room with a slight frown. "You can't live here again, Monica. It's a museum. However, if you let me—"

Monica opened the doorway of her walk-in closet. "Not now, Nikki."

Her sister sighed and let the subject drop. "What was living in that farmhouse like?"

"Wonderful," Monica said with a smile of remembrance.

"How did you spend all those months alone there?"

I wasn't alone, Monica wanted to say, but she couldn't think of JD right now. "I kept busy working on jewelry designs." She stepped farther inside and pushed a button which rotated her clothing and brought specific items to the forefront.

Nikki followed with awe, staring at the rows of shoes, accessories and designer clothing. "I could fit my apartment in your closet."

"Just help me choose something," Monica said. She had to focus. She was in no mood to humor her sister.

"What do you want to wear?"

"Something striking."

After nearly an hour they finally selected the perfect outfit for the late-summer weather then went down-

stairs and enjoyed vegetable marsala and roasted potatoes out on the patio.

Nikki set down her glass of wine. "Tell me what
you're going to do."

"The less you know the better."

"I hope you know what you're doing."

"Me, too."

Nikki raised her glass. "To taking risks."

Monica raised hers as well. "To love."

Nikki began to smile. "I wondered about that.
There's something different about you. Are you in
love?"

"Yes."

"And you can't go to him?"

"No." Monica sighed. "At least not yet."

"I hope he's worth your secrecy."

"He is."

The next three nights were a whirlwind of activities.
The cameras couldn't get enough of Venus. She decided to attend three parties in two nights and let them
flash away. When a reporter asked her about her long
absence, Monica told them a convincing story about
grieving over her husband's death and left it at that. But
Monica knew one party where she had to make an impression: Lavinia Walker's candlelight soiree. She knew
that Anton was an acquaintance of hers and she wanted
to make an entrance, so she and her sister dressed to
impress.

Nikki wore a glittering-silver floor-length dress
with a thigh-high slit while Monica selected a sweeping gown made out of embroidered damask, with flow-

ing sleeves and built-in strapless push-up bra, which afforded a clear view of her cleavage. Both women sported elegantly designed twenty-four karat gold jewelry. While Nikki selected a pair of transparent three-inch-high heels, Monica decided on a pair of two-inch strapless black patent leather heels and a pair of off-black patterned silk stockings.

Fortunately, it was a small, private affair with only fifty guests, so Monica didn't have to deal with the media and lots of absurd questions. She knew most of the guests and they were cordial. Their curiosity was evident, but they were too well mannered to pressure her to explain more than she offered.

No one wanted to upset her and they kept their distance.

"Do you see him?" Nikki asked, searching the crowd.

"No, but he'll show up. Eventually."

This was how she'd first met Anton years ago. Delong had been hosting a party after a successful gallery opening and Anton had attended. She remembered that his handshake was a bit too soft, his eyes too hard. She knew she would be able to sense he was in the room, just like any prey who understood the nature of a predator.

"There you are, Venus," Lavinia said, coming up to the two women. "I still can't believe my eyes. I'm so glad you're here."

Monica stifled a groan. Lavinia had told her that twenty times before. "I was so worried that this evening wouldn't be a success. I know that my parties are always a success, but you can still worry, you know, because anything can go wrong and I would hate for anything to go wrong even though I've given everyone strict instructions. But the fact that you're here, here in my house—I'm sure that if the rug caught fire no one would notice."

"Thank you for the invitation. I'm glad to be here. I thought it was time to see my old friends again."

"Of course! Think of us like family. I'm too young to be your mother, of course, but think of me like an aunt. I'm here for you." She looked at Nikki. "And you, too. The work you did on the Hampshire estate was divine. Absolutely divine. I want to talk to you about having my guest room redesigned."

Nikki opened her mouth to reply but Lavinia continued. "Speaking of guests, you're not the only surprise I was to have. My husband got one of his friends to come, and although I've invited him for years, he's only shown up now. And he's especially interested in meeting you." She motioned to someone to come over.

Monica resisted rolling her eyes. Someone was always interested in meeting her. "Really?" she said with forced interest. "Who?"

"JD Rozan."

Monica stiffened in shock. "He's here?"

"Funny, he had the same stunned expression when I told him about you." She clapped her hands together in delight. "Ah, there he is. Oh drats, my husband wants to talk to me. Excuse me." She hurried away, showing her obvious irritation at her husband's poor timing.

JD approached just as Lavinia was making her exit, giving Monica no means of escape. *Oh, God, he was here. What was he doing here?* She never thought he'd attend parties like this, but then again, she didn't know what his other life was like away from her. She didn't know who his friends were. What he did in his spare time. She didn't even know where he worked. Had he brought a date with him just for the sake of appearance?

He smiled and stretched out his hand. "Hello, I'm JD Rozan."

"A pleasure to meet you," Monica replied, struggling to keep her voice neutral. It was the first time she'd seen him without the shield of her tinted lens. She didn't know his brown eyes were so clear, his skin like burnished velvet. As he cast his eye over her with masculine appreciation, a part of her was thrilled and another part shriveled up. Would he recognize anything about her?

"This is my sister, Nikki."

JD redirected his attention to her. "Nikki Dupree, right?"

"Yes," her sister said, surprised that he'd recognized her.

"Lavinia was telling me about the work you've done on the Hampshire estate and I'd really like to talk to you about a job. I have a farmhouse in Georgia I'd like to make some minor changes to."

"A farmhouse?" Nikki said, sending Monica a curious look.

"Yes, I—"

"Lavinia said you wanted to see me," Monica cut in.

"Yes, sorry," JD said with a sheepish grin. "I don't want to take up your time." He released a long breath. "Wow. You're more beautiful in person than I imagined."

Monica held back a sigh. She'd hoped he would have been more creative than that. "Thank you." Soon he'd be complimenting her on her eyes and hair.

"But something's missing."

She blinked. "What?"

He pulled out a velvet attaché and held up a necklace. "I think this would be perfect."

Nikki gasped. "That looks just like—"

"It's lovely," Monica interrupted. She knew her sister recognized the pattern Monica had mimicked from their great-great-grandmother.

JD lifted a questioning brow. "May I?"

Monica nodded, and as he fastened the clasp around her neck, Nikki sent her sister a look and mouthed "Where did he get that?" Monica shook her head in a plea for her to leave it alone.

"There," JD said with a satisfied smile. "Now you're perfect."

"It's exquisite," Nikki said. "Where did you get it?"

"My girlfriend made it. She makes one-of-a-kind jewelry. She's already designed pieces for the actress Lana Davis, her royal highness Princess Denya and Julia Conrad, the new wife of multibillionaire David RH Conrad. Her popularity is quickly growing." He handed Nikki a card.

Nikki glanced down at it. "The Silver Stone?"

Monica could only stare at him. Here he was at an exclusive party surrounded by important people, and he was selling her jewelry? Then it hit her. This was how Anton had found her—through her jewelry. JD must have shown her designs to several important people and led Anton right to her.

"Did I say something wrong?" JD said, concerned. "You have a strange look on your face."

Monica quickly gathered her thoughts. "No. I'm just amazed by your girlfriend's skill."

"Yes, she's a magician. What she does will shock you."

Nikki sniffed. "You have no idea."

Monica nudged her.

JD licked his lip, taking her back to the first day he'd done that. She remembered the first time she'd been mesmerized by his full bottom lip, and now she knew what it tasted like. Her heart cried out to tell him the truth, but her mouth stayed stubbornly silent. "You once modeled my mother's creations," JD said, "and I was wondering if you would be interested in doing the same for The Silver Stone. I promise to make it worth your while. I contacted your agent, but she said you weren't accepting any new projects right now." He leaned closer and lowered his voice to a silky tone. "I'm hoping I can do something to convince you to change your mind."

"You've done well so far. I'll call you."

"Great. Now I'll leave you two." JD offered a brief smile then left.

"What's going on?" Nikki demanded in a low voice.

"I don't—" Monica's cell phone rang. She swore and quickly turned it off before JD heard the distinctive sound. She'd been carrying it with her, just in case he called, to assure him that things were okay at the farmhouse. She knew that he would come if he thought anything was wrong, but she'd forgotten to put it on vibrate.

JD came back toward them, puzzled. "Did you hear that?"

"Hear what?" Monica said.

"I could have sworn I heard…" He shook his head. "Nothing." He glanced away. "I guess I'm missing her more than I thought," he said to no one in particular.

Nikki glanced at Monica then said, "Is something wrong?"

"I've been trying to reach my girlfriend all day and I just get a busy tone. I hope she's all right."

Monica plastered on a smile. "I'm sure she is."

"She lives alone in the country. Anything can happen."

"It's late. She's probably in bed."

"Yes." He took a deep breath. "It's just that every time I'm happy, something—"

"I'm sure she's fine and she'll be happy to know you've been thinking about her."

"Right."

"Will you excuse me for a moment?" Monica asked.

"Of course."

Monica hurried into the bathroom. Nikki followed close behind. "Okay, things are getting really weird. Who is that guy?"

"JD—"

"I know his name. I mean, who is he to you? Why does he have your jewelry, and what's this about a girlfriend in the country?"

"It's complicated."

Nikki pounded her hand on the sink. "Then make it simple or I'm going to go and ask him."

"Can't you just trust me?"

"No. Now tell me what's going on. You nearly fainted when you saw him. Does he have anything to do with Anton?"

"No," she said quickly. "But he's not supposed to be here."

"Okay, so who is he and why does he have a necklace that looks just like one of your designs?"

Monica glanced up at the ceiling. "I've been seeing him."

"What?"

"As Monica Dulane. He thinks I'm a small-town jewelry maker. I've been wearing a disguise."

"Must have been one helluva disguise."

"It was. I could have fooled you."

"Well, he obviously loves you…uh…Monica Delaney."

"Dulane."

Nikki brushed away her correction. "Like it matters. You have to tell him the truth."

"That I've lied to him all these months?"

"He'll understand. God, look at you. If he doesn't understand, some other man will. You're Venus, remember?"

"I don't want another man."

"Then go out there and let him help you. He has the money to protect you."

"But who will protect him?"

"Everyone knows JD Rozan can take care of himself. His last girlfriend, Stacy Neil, even admitted in a magazine exposé to stabbing him because he helped put her father in prison. She even got a book deal out of it, but that's another story. The point is that he's a strong man. Tell him about Anton."

Monica wanted to. She knew that once JD got over the deception, he would help her. Then she thought about the fight in the alley. How he loved to win. He wouldn't just find Anton. He'd want to destroy him and in the process might be destroyed. "No, I have to handle Anton myself."

"Why?"

"Because Anton will stop at nothing."

"How do you know?"

"He killed my husband."

Chapter 16

Nikki stared at her sister, dumbfounded. "You think Delong was murdered?"

"I know he was. There's no proof, and to others it appeared that his death was an accident or suicide. His cancer was in remission and some speculated that his cancer had come back and he couldn't face it. But that wasn't it. He was in good health and looking forward to the future. He wouldn't have left me like that, and he didn't have accidents. He was very careful. Anton orchestrated it. I overheard him talking to one of the guardians, I mean my captors, that he'd offered Delong over two million dollars just to spend some time alone with me. Delong refused and Anton felt insulted, as if Delong didn't think he was good enough for me, so he took him out of the picture. He knew I had few ties and that I traveled so frequently that no one would suspect anything when I disappeared."

"You're right. Initially people wondered where you were, but we all assumed you went into seclusion, and soon everyone lost interest."

"He counted on that. Nikki, he's a dangerous man."

"So what are you going to do about JD?"

He was a complication. She had to reassure him that things were all right. "I have an idea." She opened her cell phone and dialed.

"What are you doing?"

"You'll see," she said then lightened her voice when JD picked up the line. "Hello, darling."

"Monica? I've been trying to reach you."

She wanted to rush out of the bathroom and into his arms and tell him everything, but she had to be strong. For his sake. "I know. I've been busy."

"What are you doing right now?"

She glanced around, searching for an idea. "I just finished taking a bath."

"One day that's going to be something we do together."

Monica glanced at her sister and blushed. She decided to change the subject. "You sound like you're at a party."

"Yes, I am, and I have some good news for you."

"What?"

"Venus is wearing one of your necklaces."

"Venus, the top model? I thought she'd gone into seclusion."

"She's not anymore."

"Is she beautiful?"

"She's gorgeous. How would you like a trip to the city?"

"I don't—"

"Darling, I know you're shy, but you can't miss this opportunity."

"JD, stop thinking business and just enjoy the party."

"I'll try." He hesitated. "Are things okay with you? I got a strange call from Treena."

Monica cringed. She didn't need Treena worrying about her, too. "I was just telling her that I thought I'd seen evidence of another dogfight. But I was wrong."

"I can stop by in a day or two if there's any trouble."

Her heart began to race. That was the last thing she needed. "No, I'm fine. Really."

"How about I come just to cause some trouble?" he said in a sexy, playful tone.

"Another time. Oh, I have to take something out of the oven."

"I guess I'll let you go."

"Yes, good night."

"Good night."

Monica put the cell phone back in her purse and Nikki shook her head. "You're never going to get away with this."

"I need it to work, just for tonight."

The two women left the bathroom.

"There you are!" Lavinia said, grabbing Nikki by the arm. "I have to get your opinion on my new chaise longue." She dragged Nikki away, leaving Monica alone to mingle with the rest of the crowd. After an hour she slipped into the hallway for some space away from the stares and questions. That's when she saw him. He was at the far end of the hallway. She could see

how the light glinted off his glasses. He moved toward
her and the light illuminated his features.

"Hello, Venus," Anton said.

Monica froze.

"Don't look so surprised. You knew I'd come.
I'm surprised you didn't notice me sooner. I've been
watching you all evening. Watching you with different
people, especially Rozan. Funny how he talks about his
little jewelry maker Monica all the time."

"What do you want?"

Anton's gaze traveled the length of her. "You know
what I want."

You're not going to get it. "I won't tell anyone."

"No, I'm not worried about that." He turned and
stared at the elegantly lit crowd inside the ballroom.

Monica saw his gaze focus on JD. "You leave him
alone."

Anton grinned. "Is that some kind of threat?"

"It's a warning."

"Nothing will happen, if you behave yourself."

"I have nothing to offer you. You have everything a
man could hope for."

Anton shook his head. "No, not everything. I don't
have a wife."

Monica's mouth fell open. Of everything she'd expected, she hadn't expected that. "What?"

"I've reached the age where I'm ready to settle
down." His voice deepened to huskiness and he lightly
fingered her hair. "From the first moment I saw you, I
knew I had to have you. No other woman has burned
in my heart and mind. I need you. I want you. I love

you and I have to have you. Marry me and I'll let all the others go. You'll have anything your heart desires."

"And if I don't marry you?"

"People will get hurt." He held out a piece of cloth. It was the hem of one of Lola's signature West African dresses. The look of horror on Monica's face made him smile. "It's your choice."

Monica took the cloth and traced her finger over the pattern. At least she was still alive, but for how long?

"You know where I'll be. Meet me there in two hours." He glanced at JD. "Don't forget to say goodbye," he said then left.

Monica continued to stare at the cloth. She held Lola's life in her hand, and the other women were still trapped. He wanted to marry her and then they would be set free. If she didn't...

She shoved the cloth into her purse then went and found her sister.

"I have to go."

"You saw him?" Nikki guessed, reading her sister's troubled face.

"Yes. I'll take a taxi."

"No, let me go with you."

"I have to do this alone." She wouldn't let anyone risk their life for her again.

Nikki hugged her. "Be careful."

"I will." Monica dashed into the hallway, ordered a cab and got her coat. She exited the grand house and waited outside in the circular driveway where two valets were on a smoke break, waiting for the taxicab that had been summoned.

Her phone rang. JD—again. She took a deep breath then answered. "Hello?"

"Just as I thought," a voice said behind her.

Monica spun around.

JD put his phone away, his expression unreadable. "My father told me he liked the catbird because it reminded him that things weren't always what they seemed." He stopped in front of her. "I knew you were beautiful, but never expected this."

She stared at him. "You're not mad?"

His mouth curved in a hint of a smile. "I won't be if you'll let me in on the joke."

"Joke?"

"This game you've been playing all these months."

"It's not a game and I can explain it, but not right now. There's no time."

His good humor vanished. "Are you in trouble?"

The taxi drove up and Monica marched toward it. "I really have to go."

"I'll go with you."

She held her hand out to keep him at a distance. "No."

JD took her hand and brought her close. "Monica, tell me what's going on."

"I love you more than I've loved anyone, and if you love me too, you'll let me go."

JD sighed heavily. His voice cracked with misery. "God, don't ask me to do that. Not if you're in danger."

"Please."

He cupped her face in his hands, his dark eyes filled with anguish. "Somehow I knew it was all too good to be true."

"No, it was all real. It is real. Every last bit of it." Monica kissed him, determined to make him believe her. She didn't want him to rebuild his wall against the world and she wanted to indulge in the sweetness of his lips one last time. She pulled away then repeated her plea. "Now let me go."

He tightened his grip, his voice urgent. "Just tell me—"

"I can't, Jasper Douglas."

He clenched his jaw and narrowed his eyes. "I told you never to call me that."

"I know. Are you mad enough to let me go?"

JD stared at her for a long moment then hung his head and released her. "Will you come back to me?"

"If I can, yes."

His head shot up and he searched her face but didn't ask her to explain.

Monica got into the taxi and closed the door. "Just drive," she ordered. She didn't look back as the taxi sped away.

Chapter 17

It would end tonight. Monica rode the elevator to Anton's hotel suite. He always stayed at the Madison on his visits to the city. She got to his room and knocked on the door. The door slowly swung open. She hesitated then stepped inside and removed the gun from her purse. She saw his jacket thrown over a chair. A book lay open on the dining table and the TV was on. That wasn't like him. Anton liked to leave things in order. She saw a vase overturned and went toward it but stopped when she heard footsteps coming down the hall. She ran behind a curtain and waited.

The footsteps came through the front door then hesitated. Monica peeked through the curtains and saw JD.

"What are you doing?" she demanded, coming out from her hiding place.

"I followed you."

"Why?"

He raised his brows. "Why do you think? Did you really think I'd let you go without a fight?"

Monica made a small sound of frustration. "You shouldn't be here. This is not how I planned it."

"Well, I am and you can't change that. I thought you needed my help, and I was right." He held out his hand. "Give me the gun. You killed for me once. I'll do the same for you, if I have to."

"You could go to prison."

"Better me than you." He snatched the gun from her. "What kind of trouble are you in?"

"Anton Stevens is blackmailing me. He'll kill people if I don't marry him."

"A romantic rival?"

"This is not a time for jokes."

"I'm not trying to be funny," JD said, surveying the room with a grim look. "This doesn't feel right."

"I know. I—"

He abruptly held up his hand for silence then pressed his fingers against his lips. She nodded in understanding.

He turned and walked toward the other room then a loud crash pierced the silence. Monica and JD ran toward the sound and halted in the doorway of the study. Anton lay facedown with blood seeping from his head. A woman stood over him with a gun and a silencer. She swung it around to them.

JD shoved Monica behind him. "We're not here to hurt you," he said in a gentle voice.

The gun wavered in her hand. "I had to do it."

"I know," Monica said.

The woman let the gun drop. "He killed my husband."

"I'll handle this," JD said. "Monica, get out of here."

"Why?"

"When the police come the media will soon follow. They'll swarm this place and you won't be able to leave."

"I'm not going anywhere. I'm tired of running." Monica walked over to the woman and put her arm around her. She looked dazed and in shock. "Come on and sit down."

"He killed my husband."

Monica led her to the other room. "Mine, too."

The young woman looked up at her with shining eyes. "Really? Reginald was such a good man. I was worried about the distance and how far away he'd be, but he wanted to get the money so that we could start a family. He was only there a few months before he killed him. They sent me flowers and paid for everything, but it wasn't enough. He couldn't give me my husband back. So I tracked him down. I got the name of a man they said did that sort of thing and he led me here. Now I know my life is over."

"We'll get you one of the best lawyers around," Monica said, certain that JD could find someone to help her.

Within minutes the police arrived and Alice Bower, Reginald Bower's widow, was put in handcuffs and led away. JD and Monica were also taken to the police station to give their statements. Afterward they had to duck the paparazzi, which had gotten wind of the story, by sneaking out into the alley dressed as bums. They both knew that sex, murder and revenge would sell, especially with three high-profile figures involved. Once they'd gotten to the end of the street they jumped into a waiting car that JD's associate, Cliff, had hired for them.

Gerald Hicks watched from the shadows as the car disappeared into the New York night. He'd have to get into a new line of work, but it had been worth it. He'd gotten paid and had enough money until he came up with a new situation. He couldn't let Stevens have Venus. A woman like her deserved to be free.

And Alice Bower deserved her revenge. When his cousin had asked him to find Stevens for her, he'd resisted at first until he heard the price and the reason. Stevens had made the guardians angry by disposing of one of their own so callously. They had been used to him getting rid of the girls, but when it came to one of their own, Stevens had made an error. They were like a family, and family mattered. He hoped that Alice enjoyed pulling the trigger. The guy had a lot of enemies who'd thank her for what she did.

Gerald turned from the street and thought of calling Anika to keep his bed warm, but he changed his mind. Instead, he began looking for a place to get a drink. He deserved it. He'd set a goddess free.

"When did you first suspect I was Venus?" Monica asked as Cliff drove them to a private location where the paparazzi wouldn't find them for a while.

"The moment I touched your neck," JD said, letting

his finger make a sensuous trail down it. "When I put that necklace around you, I knew."

"And you didn't say anything?" she asked in disbelief.

"I wanted to know what you were up to."

"I can't believe I didn't see it."

He sent her a sly look. "I'm also good at hiding things."

"You're sure you're not angry?"

"I was at first," JD admitted after a pause. "I couldn't believe you didn't trust me."

Monica grabbed his hand and pressed it against her chest. "I do trust you." She kissed the back of it. "I did then, too, but I was frightened. I'd seen what Anton could do, and I couldn't stand the thought of losing you."

JD's gaze roamed over her face, as if he still couldn't believe she was real. "The moment you came into my life, I was a new man. It took me a while to recognize it, but I know it now. You taught me that happiness is a choice and that I have to fight to keep it. Letting it go is the easy way out, and I finally understood what my father and grandmother wanted for me. But I want you to learn something from me. I want you to know that you never have to be afraid again. You're always safe with me. To me you're a treasure worth dying for, and I'd give my life for you without hesitation."

His ardent words shook Monica to her core and frightened her a little. It was too much of a sacrifice. "And I'll die for you."

JD shook his head. "No, I want you to do something my father asked of me."

"What?"

He gathered her close. "Live for me."

Chapter 18

They made love that night and kept all the lights on.

Anton's empire crumbled and the men who benefited from his services scattered like cockroaches. Most of the guardians disappeared before the compound was seized. All the women he'd kept were released and their story made international headlines. Some were eager to tell their stories, while others disappeared and chose to remain hidden.

Monica made provisions so that Lola could come see her in America. She met Lola at the airport, and when the two women saw each other they rushed into each other's arms and cried.

"This is all because of you," Monica said through her tears.

"No," Lola said in a hoarse whisper. "The moment you left, I was free."

Monica stared at her in shock. They were Lola's first words after nearly two years of silence. Monica didn't know what to say, so all she did was hug her again to let her know she was safe now.

Lola decided to stay with Monica in Georgia (although Nikki offered to let her stay with her) while JD took care of business in the city. Lola loved the town and she soon started to volunteer at the local animal shelter and help with various fundraisers. She related to the animals in a special way no one else did, and everybody believed that she had a gift of making scared animals feel calm.

Back at his apartment, Donnie helped JD pack some things he planned to keep at the farmhouse.

Once it was all done, JD treated his little brother to a beer and said, "Thanks."

"No problem," Donnie said with a nonchalant shrug. He took a long swallow.

"No, not for the packing. For staying out of trouble."

"Oh, that."

"Yes, *that*. You were becoming a nuisance."

He grinned. "But I made your life exciting, right?"

"I don't need that kind of excitement," JD said in a grim voice.

"I know. And you have better things to do with your time than help me out of scrapes. Don't worry. I'm on the straight and narrow now."

"When you lie like that it makes me nervous."

Donnie laughed. "Okay, maybe my path's just a little crooked, but it's nothing for you to worry about."

"Good."

He took a sip of his drink. "A woman like Monica could make a man rethink his ways. She could help me—"

JD directed his drink at him. "Don't even think about it."

"Hey, we're going to be related, right? What's wrong with me asking her for a little sisterly advice?"

JD set his drink down and gripped him in a playful choke hold. "Say that again?"

"I'm kidding. I'm kidding."

"Let's come to an agreement. You stay out of trouble and stay away from Monica for at least a year until I know I can trust you. Agreed?"

Donnie nodded.

JD released him and patted him on the back. "Glad to hear it."

Donnie was quiet a moment then said in a serious tone, "I'm glad things worked out for you. Gran was always afraid you'd end up alone." He finished off his drink then set it aside. "You remember Dad a lot more than I do, and I've always felt that you keep him alive."

JD looked at him in surprise. "No, not me. You're more like him than I am. He could make people laugh and he had charisma like you."

"But he was smart too and great at business."

"Yes. I guess we're both keeping him alive then."

Donnie nodded, liking the idea. He raised his drink in a toast. "To Dad."

JD raised his own drink. "Yes, and to us."

JD and Monica got married at the farmhouse. Although they both could have afforded a big, showy event, they chose to keep it quiet and simple. The ceremony was short but the reception was not. Guests dined on sumptuous dishes and cool drinks into the early evening.

"I thought Nadine was crazy when she rented this farmhouse," Crystalline said to Monica as the two women stood outside the grand structure that had been decorated for the occasion. "But I guess she knew what she was doing, especially when she selected you. You were meant to be here."

"Oh, no, she was just desperate. She told me I was the only one interested."

Crystalline shook her head with a knowing smile. "That may be what she told you, but there were others. The Wooley brothers offered to continue to manage the place for her. She refused, and when you showed up she knew why. She knew that you belonged here." She cupped Monica's chin. "You are a luck child, aren't you?"

Monica hesitated, surprised by the question. "My parents thought so."

"And they were right. Your beauty shines so bright because your spirit is pure. My husband once said that someone born under a lucky star would come here and change our lives. I never believed him, but now I do."

Monica shook her head, not wanting to take credit. "No, I didn't change anyone's life. You changed mine. I never realized how much I missed belonging to a family."

Crystalline took her hand. "Daughter, from now on you will never be alone." She lightly kissed her on the cheek then left.

Monica touched her cheek, now realizing how much she'd missed being someone's daughter.

Nikki rushed up to her. "This place is fabulous! When you told me you were staying in a farmhouse, I was thinking of some dilapidated shack that smelled like horses and hay."

"That would be a barn."

Nikki dismissed her. "Like it matters. This place is amazing. No wonder you wanted to stay here. The architecture is stellar and the carpentry…"

Monica laughed at her sister's enthusiasm. "I know. I know."

"I have so many ideas I want to give JD about this place. I think it's a great idea that you two will spend most of your time here."

JD was ready to try something new and wanted to help the local businesses prosper. For the first time in her life she had a place that was hers. Monica looked at Donnie making Lola laugh and Treena sipping drinks with another guest. She no longer felt like an outsider. She wasn't strange or different. She was home.

"What are you thinking, Mrs. Rozan?" JD asked, coming up behind her.

"How wonderful all of this is."

"It will get even better."

He bent down to kiss her, but someone cleared his throat. They both turned and saw Treena's husband, William.

"Sorry to interrupt," he said, embarrassed. "But could I have a word?" he asked JD.

Monica slipped away and JD looked at him

and waited. He'd been surprised that William had even come.

William cleared his throat. "I just wanted to say that I'm sorry about what I'd said last summer."

"Forget it. I understand. I didn't write like I said I would."

"It wasn't that. I was jealous." He glanced at Monica, who was now talking to three of the waitstaff. "You've always been a lucky SOB."

"I know it."

William laughed. "Yeah, that's what pissed me off. You were always so sure of yourself. Confident that things would go your way, and they always did."

"No," he said, remembering the death of his father. "Not always."

William remembered too and sobered. "He would have been proud of you." He shoved his hands in his pockets. "I guess that's it then."

"How's business?"

"It's still bad."

"Can I offer you some advice, or are you going to bite my head off again?"

"This time I'll keep my mouth shut. I'm open to any advice you can give me."

JD patted him on the back. "I'll get in touch with you."

"Thanks," William said then went to rejoin his wife.

The sound of a helicopter filled the evening sky and everyone looked up and watched it land in the back field. JD went to gather his new bride.

"Looks like our ride's here," he said, taking her hand. Donnie and Lola handed them their luggage.

"Where are you taking me?" Monica asked as JD opened the door.

"First, to an exclusive hotel."

"And then?" Monica asked as he climbed in behind her and locked his seat belt.

"I have a friend who couldn't attend, but he owns a private island in the Mediterranean. Darling, I'm taking you to paradise."

Monica wrapped her arms around him, joy shining in her eyes. "I feel like I'm already there."

They returned from paradise with a beautiful souvenir.

"A baby? I get to be an aunt?" Nikki squealed on the phone.

"Yes," Monica laughed, pleased with her sister's delight.

"You have to let me decorate the nursery. Please."

"Okay," Monica said then nearly regretted the idea when Nikki came down to visit and share her ideas.

"Don't you think you're overdoing it a bit?" Monica asked, looking at some of her sister's sketches.

Nikki surveyed the guest room she'd selected to be the nursery and waved her sister away. "I never go overboard."

"But—"

Nikki gently pushed Monica out of the room. "Just trust me. You're going to love it." She closed the door.

Monica shrugged her shoulders, resigned. Her sister had never disappointed her before, and she didn't expect that to change. She went into her studio and worked for the next couple of hours on one piece but stopped and rubbed her lower back. It was getting more and more difficult to do some of her more intricate pieces with her stomach in the way. Monica washed her hands in the sink then halted and looked at herself in the full-length mirror.

At first she wasn't sure who she saw. She definitely didn't see sexy Venus with her killer figure and provocative beauty, but she also didn't see dumpy Monica Dulane in her dull, loose clothes, hiding behind tinted glasses. What she saw was a woman beaming with good health and happily married (although she'd had to take off her wedding ring). She looked forward to wearing the ring JD had had designed for her again after the baby was born.

Monica slid her hand over the curve of her belly. *The baby.* That changed it. She'd no longer be in men's fantasies. That status had been a source of strength and power for her at one time, and she had to let it go. She released a sigh of acceptance. She'd found she had strength in other ways, and she wouldn't give up the life she and JD had created. But she couldn't deny that her image had become a part of her and it was strange to see it disappear.

"Venus has left the building," Monica said to her reflection as she cast a critical eye over her expanding figure.

"What?" JD asked, coming into the room.

She glanced at him over her shoulder. "I was just saying that Venus is gone."

JD came up behind her and wrapped his arms around her waist, resting his hands on the curve of her stomach. "I don't need a goddess. I like my women real."

Monica raised an eyebrow. "And just how many women do you have?"

"One's enough for me."

"Hmm." She leaned back against him, covering his hand with her own. "You better enjoy this moment, because you soon won't be able to hold me like this for a while."

JD kissed her on the neck and whispered, "I'll always find a way to hold you."

Monica laughed and turned to him. "You're going to have to be real creative, because I'm only six months and I've already gained—"

JD stopped her with another kiss, this time on the mouth, and his persuasive lips swept away all her worries. When he finally drew away he said, "You just get more beautiful every time I look at you. I told you before—" he pointed to the ground "—in this room that I thought you were wonderful." He lifted her chin with his forefinger and gazed into her eyes with love. "And that will never change."

The newest arrival to the Rozan family made her appearance in the spring. She had a head full of ink-black hair and her father's brown eyes. Crystalline wanted to call her Sapphire, Nikki thought that Nina had a nice ring and Donnie felt that Dawn would be perfect. But JD and Monica settled on Starla. She was born on a day that the azalea bushes came into full bloom, the breeze lifting their fragrance into the air, and she delighted all who saw her. She made her grandmother cry, her uncle laugh and her aunt sigh. Her parents just gazed at her with amazement.

She was a happy baby who loved to be rocked to sleep by her mother while her father played a soft lullaby on his guitar with the family dog curled up on the handmade knotted rug by his feet.

Monica looked at her husband, and his steady gaze showed her the pleasure of joy, the harmony of peace and the unwavering beauty of love.

* * * * *

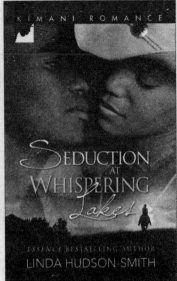

REQUEST YOUR FREE BOOKS!

2 FREE NOVELS
PLUS 2 FREE GIFTS!

KIMANI ROMANCE ™

Love's ultimate destination!

KROM11B